The Christmas Pig

A Fable

KINKY FRIEDMAN

SIMON & SCHUSTER

New York · London · Toronto · Sydney

SIMON & SCHUSTER
Rockefeller Center
1230 Avenue of the Americas
New York, NY 10020

SIMON & SCHUSTER and colophon are registered trademarks
of Simon & Schuster, Inc.

For information about special discounts for bulk purchases,
please contact Simon & Schuster Special Sales at
1-800-456-6798 or business@simonandschuster.com

DESIGNED BY LAUREN SIMONETTI

Manufactured in the United States of America

1 3 5 7 9 10 8 6 4 2

Library of Congress Cataloging-in-Publication Data
Friedman, Kinky.
The Christmas pig: a fable / Kinky Friedman
p. cm
1. Christmas stories.
PS3556.R527C47 2006
813'.54—dc22   2006051200

ISBN-13: 978-1-4516-4338-1

Acknowledgments

The author would like to thank Elizabeth Coatsworth, Oscar Wilde, Anna Louise Drinkall, Issy Drinkall, Max Swafford, Jay Wise, David Rosenthal, David Vigliano, and, of course, Ben and Valerie.

For Rita Jo
Always my Miss Texas

The Christmas Pig

CHAPTER ONE

Where Are Feinberg's Shoes?

H E WAS A GOOD king but he was in a bad mood. Christmas was only a month away and he still had not commissioned an artist to paint the traditional nativity scene to be unveiled at the conclusion of the midnight mass.

"I've crushed whole armies for not celebrating Christmas," complained the king to his chief advisor, Feinberg. "Now I can't even properly celebrate it myself. Is there not an artist left in the kingdom? Have they all been burned at the stake?"

"Nay, my liege," said Feinberg. "They certainly have *not* all been burned at the stake. Some of them have merely starved to death."

1

"I see," said the king, which, of course, was unlikely. That was because he was a king and not an artist.

Still, he was a good king, as kings go. His name was Jonjo Mayo the First, and, as fate would have it, he would also be the last. As history marched inexorably by, his tiny kingdom would be gobbled up and spit out repeatedly by the Pagans, the Vandals, the Arabs, and eventually, that group that always had considered itself less savage than the other savages, the Christians. Today, sadly, the kingdom can no longer be found on any map. Its boundaries, its nooks and crannies, its very heart and soul have been incorporated by a large, gray, boring country. Indeed, the entire reign of King Jonjo Mayo the First might have been forgotten completely had it not been for the fortuitous intervention of a small silent boy and a pig.

Feinberg, like practically all advisors to royalty, came from mysterious, humble origins. Thus it was that he was not particularly facile in his relations with the knights, noblemen, and other members of the court aristocracy. Indeed, he regarded them as useful idiots, which, indubitably, most of them were. They often mocked Feinberg's eccentricities, of which there were many, and his social skills, of which there were few. Feinberg encouraged this by providing them with various odd behaviors such as occasionally appearing in formal court without his shoes. Whenever these supposed incidents of absentmindedness occurred, King Jonjo would invariably rush to the defense of his advisor like a mother duck to a wayward duckling.

"Where are Feinberg's shoes?" the king would thunder from the throne.

The members of the court would then mutter dutifully amongst themselves for several moments until at last Feinberg himself would make a great show of looking down and pretending to suddenly realize that his feet were bare.

"Whosoever has taken Feinberg's shoes shall return them immediately!" shouted King Jonjo. "All of you! Out of my sight until Feinberg's shoes have been found and reunited with Feinberg's feet!"

The entire court aristocracy would then scurry hither and thither around the castle under the stern displeasure of the king and, of course, the private enjoyment of Feinberg. Feinberg knew with a certainty that without King Jonjo there would be no Feinberg. On the other foot, the king realized that without Feinberg, there would probably be no one there to follow his orders to search for Feinberg's shoes.

By the time the disgruntled courtiers returned empty-handed, they were further chagrined to find that Feinberg's feet were no longer bare. Not only had the advisor to the throne, mysteriously, perhaps magically, located his shoes, he'd also come up with another harebrained idea that was sure to please the king.

"Your majesty," said Feinberg, when the court had reassembled. "I know of an artist who may just be able to produce the nativity painting in time for the midnight mass."

The court mumbled and rumbled in reaction to this new brainstorm, particularly the small group of noblemen who had been discussing it within earshot

4

of Feinberg, but had been afraid to set it forth themselves before the king.

"Who is this man?" said the king.

"He is not a man, your highness," said Feinberg, as the court giggled and sniggled around him.

"When is an artist not a man?" asked the king, somewhat rhetorically. Every time he asked a question, it had the effect of being rhetorical.

"An artist is not a man," said Feinberg, pausing for dramatic effect, "when the artist is a *child*."

The king gasped. The court gasped. The king looked at Feinberg. The court looked at Feinberg. Feinberg looked down at his shoes. They were nowhere to be seen, however. His feet once again were bare.

"You are suggesting," said King Jonjo rather incredulously, "that I commission a *child* to paint the nativity scene for the midnight mass on Christmas Eve?"

"Who better than a child, your highness," reasoned Feinberg, "to paint a child?"

"It's ridiculous, your majesty," shouted a nobleman.

5

"It's blasphemous!" shouted another.

"And so it is," said the king. "But I admit to being rather taken with the idea. Just who *is* this child?"

"A ten-year-old boy, my liege," said Feinberg. "From a small village along the northern coastline. He's considered to be a magical boy. Never spoken a word in his life, but paints like a dream."

"Bring him to me," said the king.

CHAPTER TWO

The Mermaid

WITH A GREAT CLATTER of hooves and the blare of trumpets, three knights rode out of the castle that afternoon on commission from the king. The gravity of their task did not evade them. King Jonjo was a stickler on matters of tradition. If the magical boy did not exist, for example, or if they couldn't find him and fetch him to the court in a timely fashion, there could be hell to pay.

"I could strangle Feinberg with my own hands," said the Black Knight, as he rode through the drizzle toward the northern coastline.

"He has the auditory prowess of a blind man," said

7

the White Knight. "He hears every whisper in the court."

"Aye," said the Gray Knight, as he reined his horse away from another large puddle of muddy water. "But this grand experiment may yet come to be known as Feinberg's Folly. Commissioning a mere child to create a work of such import and magnitude could well serve to humiliate the royal court. If ill-conceived or biblically inaccurate it could make King Jonjo the laughingstock of all Christendom."

"One never wishes ill to the king, of course," said the White Knight, "but at least it would put an end to Feinberg and his bloody shoes."

"Hear! Hear!" shouted the Black Knight, as he inadvertently galloped through a large puddle, splashing all three well-turned-out riders with muddy, freezing water.

The journey took the better part of the day and some of the night and it was pissing down rain by the time they arrived at their destination. The place was called Long Lama, a small, desolate farming and fishing community that had been slowly dying for more than a hundred years. Long Lama was quite off the beaten path and none of the three had ever been there before. Their fervent hope was that they would never be there again.

They put up for the night at the only place they could find, a dreary-looking little affair named The Mermaid. Deep inside the storm and the darkness they could hear the fateful, foreboding sounds of the sea crashing, unfriendly and unbidden, close within the narrow crawl space of their aristocratic souls. They no longer looked like royal messengers for the king as they handed over the reins of their horses to a big fellow with an unkempt red beard who gave every appearance of being a Viking just off the ship.

"We're on commission from the king," said the White Knight to the Viking.

"Right ye are, my lord," said the big man winking broadly. "And I was just having tea with the Duchess of Shitesbury."

"Ever hear of a magical boy who lives around here?" asked the Black Knight. "Some consider him to be quite the artist?"

"Hear of him?" said the Viking indignantly. "Found the little bugger myself! Found him in a wee basket on me doorstep on a stormy night like this some ten years back it was. Some say a mermaid brought him in from the sea."

"And some say the boy has never spoken," said the White Knight. "Is that correct?"

"I have never heard him speak as you and I speak, my lord."

"So the boy is retarded?"

The Viking laughed heartily as he finished putting the horses up for the night. He continued to chuckle to himself as he led the noblemen to their quarters.

"There are two kinds of sailors," said the Viking at last. "The sailor who fights the sea, and the sailor who loves the sea. The lad is retarded only to them who do not realize he is a genius."

"I see," said the White Knight, which, of course, was unlikely. That was because he was a nobleman and not a Viking.

The three travelers weathered a drafty, rather sleepless night, with the raw power of the sea pounding relentlessly into their waking and sleeping senses. During the long course of the night they each experienced strange and strikingly similar dreams, which, being bound by aristocratic bloodlines, they did not choose to share with one another in the morning. The dream was of a lighthouse-keeper and an extremely vivid, passionate union he once consummated with a mermaid.

CHAPTER THREE

The Bridge

BEING A KNIGHT is not all it's sometimes cracked up to be. From cradle to grave they see nothing but the dank, barren insides of castle walls, empty suits of armor, the wrong end of catapults, and walk-in closets filled with uncomfortable, ridiculous wardrobes they are compelled to wear. Born into the aristocracy, they become the most culture-bound of all human beings and then suddenly, without merit or crime, real people in the real world are thrust with careless abandon upon their delicate sensitivities and misguided value systems. And, to add to that, no one had seen a dragon in several centuries.

Thus it was that the three emissaries from the

king, in all their mud-splattered royal finery, after a fine breakfast of kippers, rode out of The Mermaid the next morning in search of a child who could not speak. Conversing amongst themselves, they were beginning to wonder if the journey was going to be worth it. Accustomed as they were to doing the bidding of the king, they were, nonetheless, highly doubtful that this little adventure would ever, indeed, bring glory to the court or to themselves.

"What balderdash!" muttered the Black Knight. "A *child* painting a *child*."

"Maybe that is the method in the madness," reasoned the Gray Knight.

"Of course, one hates to wish ill upon the king," offered the White Knight.

"That, my friend, is exactly what I fear shall happen," said the Black Knight. "The king will be made to look the fool. Then he will seek vengeance upon those closest to his majesty."

"And that, unfortunately," concluded the White Knight, "appears to be us."

With a sense of almost palpable foreboding hanging over their noble heads, a situation that was not alleviated by the gloomy and threatening heavens above, the three chanced upon a small wooden bridge over a shallow ravine. Crossing the bridge in single file, they came upon a dark, hooded figure standing in their path. The spectral being appeared to be that of an old man holding a scythe.

"What riders are ye?" he shrieked in an eerie, birdlike voice.

The noblemen glanced nervously at one another. This was a character they had never encountered in their fortunate and somewhat shallow lives.

"We come from the king," shouted the White Knight at last.

"There is no king," said the wizened old man. "There is only the imagination of a child."

"He is a blasphemous old fool," said the Black Knight to the others. "Still, he may be able to help us."

But before he could address the old man further, the ghostly creature advanced upon them. He came very close indeed but they still could not discern his face.

"What do you want with the magical boy?" said the man on the bridge.

The riders exchanged startled glances. Could this faceless old codger read their minds?

"We want to bring the magical boy to the king," said the White Knight.

"There is no king," said the man on the bridge. "There is only the love of a friend."

"Maybe there is no magical boy," said the Gray Knight.

"The magical boy lives," said the wraithlike figure.

"He may live," said the Black Knight, "but you will die now, old man."

With that, the three riders spurred their steeds directly toward the man on the bridge. Suddenly, the air became very cold and the daylight around them vanished into darkness. Oddly enough, the horsemen could not seem to make physical contact with the man on the bridge. They had seemingly ridden right through the ancient fellow, and yet, there he was, still standing on the bridge.

"Why didn't he die?" the Gray Knight asked aloud.

"I am Death," said the man on the bridge.

CHAPTER FOUR

The Magical Boy

IFE ALWAYS SEEMS full of promise after a brush with Death and so the three emissaries now redoubled their efforts to find the magical boy. Indeed, following the Viking's simple directions, it was not long before they came upon the small, rather dilapidated farm they took to be their destination. They were greeted by a skinny farmhand and a skinny dog. The farmhand, who resembled a young Don Quixote, introduced himself as Will Wallace.

"We are sent from the king," said the White Knight, "to find the magical boy."

"You have come to the right place," said Will Wallace. "Just now, unfortunately, the lad is eating his oatmeal and cannot be disturbed."

The knights exchanged quizzical glances as the farmhand then proceeded to usher them into a clean, if rather humble, living room. They could hear the voices of a man and a woman murmuring in the nearby little kitchen.

"Just what is so magical about this magical lad?" the Black Knight inquired of the farmhand.

"He can paint your dreams," said the farmhand.

"I see," said the Black Knight, but, of course, he did not.

A few moments later, as the farmhand was bowing his way out, an elderly couple entered the room and introduced themselves. The farmer and his wife were understandably curious as to why three men garbed in such mud-splattered refinement were currently gracing their living room.

"Welcome to our little farm," said Uncle Floyd Welch, the farmer.

"Is there anything we can get you?" asked his wife, Aunt Joan.

"We have come to see the magical boy," said the

White Knight. "We are here to take him to the court of King Jonjo the First."

"Benjamin cannot travel, your lordships," said the wife, casting a worried look into the kitchen and moving slightly closer to her husband. "We are not his true parents but we took him in as a babe and since then he has never set foot outside our little farm."

"Benjamin thinks of us as his Aunt Joan and Uncle Floyd," said the farmer, "but the truth is he has no known blood relatives. He was a gift to us and, as you may know, he has a great gift as an artist. That, I presume, is how his majesty became aware of Benjamin."

"That is correct, sir," said the Black Knight. "The king is desirous of paying Benjamin a very substantial commission to paint the traditional nativity scene to be formally unveiled at the conclusion of the midnight mass on Christmas Eve."

"Well," said Uncle Floyd, "I won't say we couldn't use the money. We're deeply in debt and could well run the risk of losing our little farm."

"Dear," said Aunt Joan firmly to her husband, "I

won't allow this to happen. The boy is unable to travel and even if he could make the trip, he is unable to speak to the king."

"The boy does not speak," Uncle Floyd confided to the knights.

"The boy does not have to speak to the king," the Black Knight intoned. "The king, however, has commanded that the boy appear before him. And so it shall be."

Aunt Joan took out a small handkerchief and began to quietly weep. Uncle Floyd put his arm around her shoulders protectively. The knights retired to a corner and conferred amongst themselves. In the kitchen, the magical boy continued to eat his oatmeal. Unlike most small boys, Benjamin liked oatmeal. He did not like small boys, however. This, very possibly, was because of the fact that he had never met one.

Indeed, the only three human beings the little lad had interacted with in the course of his young life had been Uncle Floyd, Aunt Joan, and Will Wallace, the farmhand. He spent his time reading, walking alone in the nearby woods, or painting in the old barn, which Aunt Joan liked to refer to as his studio. He did not even feel any particular closeness to the dog or the cat or the other animals on the little farm. He was a magical boy all alone in his lonely, magical world. And now he had finished his oatmeal.

"Well, well," said the White Knight, as Benjamin unwittingly walked into the room, "here's the young lad now."

Benjamin stopped and rocked slightly as if he were standing on the edge of a cliff. He had not seen men like these before and now one of them was holding out his hand to him. Benjamin had witnessed his Uncle Floyd occasionally shaking hands with other men, but he had never willingly touched another person in his life. He did not do so now. In fact, he stood perfectly still, listening to the rain begin to fall on the straw roof.

The Knight withdrew his proffered hand and observed the young lad more closely. He was small for his age. Red hair. Eyes blue as a robin's egg. And those unearthly blue eyes were staring right at him. Nay, they were staring right *through* him. They were staring into the very depths of his soul, which,

21

in this case, amounted to a fairly short journey. Nonetheless, it served to make the courtier mildly uncomfortable.

"Why is he just standing there?" said the knight. "Can he hear me?"

"Of course he hears you," said Aunt Joan. "He is not deaf."

"Then why does he keep staring at me?"

"Maybe he wants to paint your dreams," she said.

Moments later, the strange redheaded lad had disappeared as abruptly as he had arrived. The three gentlemen from the court had been conferring again in the corner of the room and when they looked up, he was gone.

"The kid appears and vanishes almost as quickly as Feinberg's shoes," said the White Knight.

"The kid gives me the creeps," said the Black Knight.

"Get used to it," said the Gray Knight. "We're taking him back to the court with us."

It was beginning to rain a little harder now, but Uncle Floyd seemed determined to show his courtly visitors the lad's work. When his guests discovered that the piece of art in question resided in the nearby barn, they at first balked at the idea. Finally, reasoning among themselves, they decided that their elegant plumage was already a drooping mess and a short dash to the barn would have little effect upon their wounded vanities. They also felt, quite logically, that before they proceeded to drag this odd lad halfway across the kingdom, they ought to at least discover for themselves some evidence that he could actually paint.

They navigated their way through the rain to the old barn, the White Knight helping the old farmer, the Black Knight cursing every puddle he stepped in, and the Gray Knight seemingly becoming one with the color of the rain. At last they came to the old decrepit barn, which felt as damp and dank as a lighthouse except there was no light. The old structure creaked and howled with every gust of wind and the musty smells of the barnyard animals were somewhat stifling. Finally, Uncle Floyd lighted a lantern

23

and they saw a skinny brown cow, an old white, swaybacked horse, a dirty lost-looking little lamb, a balding old rooster, a thin, lazy-looking brown dog, an angry-looking black cat, and a runty little brown and white pig.

"Fine menagerie you have here," said the White Knight.

"They look like rejects from Noah's Ark," muttered the Black Knight.

"Where's the kid's painting?" said the Gray Knight.

Uncle Floyd led the three knights deeper into the gloomy old barn where they saw a small easel and a little wooden chair. As the farmer held the lantern up to Benjamin's most recent work, the three intrepid travelers peered intensely at it with an equal mixture of horror and disbelief.

"And you say the lad has never been off the farm?" asked the White Knight incredulously.

"That's why I worry about the journey to the court," said Uncle Floyd. "Benjamin's never set foot off this place in his life."

The painting was a precise replication of the little

wooden bridge near the town of Long Lama. The same bridge the riders had traversed earlier that morning. Standing on the bridge was a hooded figure holding a scythe. Under the hood, the figure had no face. Only a skull.

CHAPTER FIVE

Leaving Home

BY LATE THAT EVENING the emissaries from the king were uncomfortably ensconced at The Mermaid, having safely traversed the little bridge on the road to Long Lama without meeting Death. The bridge bore an almost uncanny resemblance to the one in Benjamin's painting, so much so that they'd ridden across it rather quickly and gingerly. Now they were seated by a small fireplace in the little pub drinking pints of bitter and negotiating with the Viking over a small cart sturdy enough to carry the boy and his uncle to the court of King Jonjo.

"That cart will slow us down a great deal," said the White Knight, "but clearly the boy cannot travel alone with us. I'm not even sure it gives him enough time to finish the painting by Christmas."

"Don't worry," said the Black Knight. "He's a fast worker, according to his mother."

"She's not his mother," said the Gray Knight, with a mischievous smile. "His mother, remember, was a mermaid."

"Aye," said the Viking, staring somberly into the fire.

"And what, pray tell," asked the White Knight of the Viking, "was your occupation before you became the proprietor of this establishment?"

"I was a sailor, sir," said the Viking, as he continued to stare into the flames. "Then for a time I was a lighthouse-keeper."

Each knight privately remembered his own vivid dream of the night before. Each knight quietly reflected upon the Viking's red beard and the red-haired lad they'd soon be accompanying to the court. Collectively, the three knights felt a chill run swiftly up and down their chivalrous spines.

"Be gentle with that lad," said the Viking. "He paints with a steady hand, a clear head, and a singing heart. But what the lad may paint today, so I am told, may well become your tomorrow."

The next morning, according to the agreement the knights had made with the Welch family, Uncle Floyd, Aunt Joan, and the boy, Benjamin, showed up at The Mermaid in a flimsy wooden trap pulled by the old white mare. Fortunately for all concerned, neither the old mare, the broken-down trap, nor the frail and somewhat emotional Aunt Joan would be traveling to the court. It was a daunting journey for the most hardened of travelers under the best conditions. Someone from the family had to accompany the boy and someone had to stay behind to help run the farm. The road was not a friendly place for women or children. Nevertheless, Aunt Joan remained quite concerned about the boy leaving home.

"Now, dear," said Uncle Floyd soothingly, "we can't keep the lad on the farm with the critters forever. It is time for him to see the real world."

"Why," asked Aunt Joan quite reasonably, "must anybody have to see the real world?"

This was a question the farmer could not readily answer, as he took the boy's little suitcase out of the flimsy trap and placed it into the sturdy wagon bound for the road. The boy sat next to his aunt and did not appear to be prepared to be going anywhere.

"Don't forget that this is a great opportunity for Benjamin's talents to shine," said Uncle Floyd. "It is also the only chance we have to keep the farm from being taken away from us. If that were to happen, we'd all have to live in the real world."

"At least we'd be together," said Aunt Joan.

The three knights and the Viking observed this little drama not unkindly as they prepared the horses and the wagon. None of them had ever had his own family and, knowing the ways of the real world as they did, they each knew it was unlikely that they ever would. Instead of wives, they would have their journeys. Instead of children, they would have their dreams. The real world, they had learned, was not so good and not so bad after all.

For his part, Benjamin could not take his eyes off

the Viking. The knights, even with their newly refurbished colorful plumage, held little interest for him. The town of Long Lama likewise did not seem to pique his curiosity. Nor did he appear eager to leave his place beside his Aunt Joan to mount the wagon with his Uncle Floyd. No amount of coaxing was able to move the magical boy.

"We're off to rather a slow start," remarked the Gray Knight wryly, as he fastened the girth of his horse.

"Come, Benjamin," said Uncle Floyd, as he patted the seat beside him in the wagon. "This is a chance to show the world your talents, my lad."

Benjamin did not glance at his uncle. He instead watched the Viking as the burly, bearded man strode purposefully back into the pub.

"Come on, Benjamin," said Aunt Joan encouragingly as she got up and walked over to the larger conveyance. "See, I'm placing a large bag of oatmeal into the wagon for you."

The boy did not move a muscle. He sat alone on the seat of the small wooden cart like the stubborn, petulant young child that he was. But in his mind there was neither stubbornness nor petulance. In his mind was a thought he could not have articulated to another human being. The thought was, *There is a light shining over the waves.*

"Shite!" said the Black Knight. "We may have to transfer the little bugger by force."

"I wouldn't try that if I were you," said the White Knight. "The lad might gaze at you with those strange blue eyes and decide he wants to paint you as the court jester."

"Which is what all three of us will become," said the Gray Knight, "if we don't deliver him to King Jonjo pretty quickly."

The situation, however, was soon to be remedied. The Viking came storming out of the pub with his red hair flaming behind him and his big beard bustling and moved toward the larger conveyance in which Benjamin's uncle was already sitting. In the Viking's large hands was a small tablet.

"Now, my lad, I have sailed the seas of this globe but never have I been privileged to travel on a journey over the land for all the miles you are about to undertake. I have only gone part of the way.

"In my hands I hold this sketchbook in which I have never sketched a whit because, of course, I cannot draw. Will you do a favor for me, lad? Will you sketch for me the things you see on this great journey? I must stay here with The Mermaid. But you can bring me back the people, the animals, the towns, the wondrous sights that your eyes will see so that I, too, may see them upon your return. Will you do that for me, my lad?"

Without further coaxing, the boy slid off the seat of the small trap and climbed aboard the wagon next to his uncle. The Viking handed Benjamin the blank sketchpad along with a pencil but he did not attempt to touch the boy. Indeed, he already had.

CHAPTER SIX

The Journey

WITH TEARS IN HER EYES, Aunt Joan waved goodbye as two strong horses pulled the cart carrying Floyd and Benjamin on the long journey to the royal court. The White Knight led the little procession while the Black Knight and the Gray Knight rode alongside the wagon, almost as if they believed their precious young passenger might try to make a break for it. It was, indeed, the furthest thing from Benjamin's mind. He had not even waved goodbye to his Aunt Joan. He had not, of course, ever waved goodbye to anyone.

Uncle Floyd was a very strong and positive-thinking man. As he smiled and waved goodbye to

KINKY FRIEDMAN

his wife, he fully believed the pilgrimage to the court of King Jonjo would be a great success. The boy was exceedingly talented. This much he knew for sure. The amount of the commission of which the knights had spoken would be just about enough to bail his little family out of debt and save the farm from foreclosure. But this was nothing, thought Uncle Floyd, as the wagon jolted and swayed its way out of the town of Long Lama, compared to what this journey might mean for Benjamin's future. If the king liked the boy's work and became his patron, the young lad could be assured of fame and fortune for the rest of his life.

But as Aunt Joan patted the old white mare and watched the cart with Benjamin roll out of sight, she was not so sure. He was a good boy, she knew that. He also had a blindingly brilliant talent that, she supposed, should not be hidden from the world. On the other hand, she feared very much that that same world might destroy her son.

And yes, she did consider the boy to be her son even though she quite well knew he wasn't. He was a child of the dust and the rain and the sea. Sometimes she almost believed he'd never had a mother. He seemed like such an ancient soul, carved out of the Rock of Ages and given to her by God Himself.

So different from other little boys, she thought wistfully, as she headed back toward the farm. Even as a babe, he'd never laughed, never cried. In his ten years of life on this green earth, she realized, she'd never witnessed any display of emotion at all from the child she and her husband had named Benjamin. And yet, he was so sensitive in his odd way, so intuitive. He didn't miss a thing that was going on around him, his paintings showed that. He just could not or would not communicate with any other living soul. He was not kind or unkind, polite or impolite, sad or happy. He was none of the things you might say about a young boy. He was like a star, so far away you could never tell what he was thinking, so close you could almost touch him.

And yet. And yet she knew he loved her. She knew like every mother knows and every lover knows, even if it is not true. He was a good lad with a good heart, wise beyond his years from reading and watching his little world go by. It was all there, all right. All there inside his unknowable mind like so much undigested food for thought. Did he love her the way she loved him? Probably not, she suspected. Maybe Benjamin didn't love. Maybe Benjamin was love.

Benjamin liked the Gray Knight the best. This had nothing whatsoever to do with the knight himself or the manner in which he'd interacted with Benjamin. Gray was merely the world in which Benjamin lived, the color with which he was the most comfortable. And colors, as any artist will tell you, are the brick and mortar of survival in an essentially colorless world. Gray, of course, is rather unusual. It would not be the color most artists or most people would pick as their favorite. It is an in-between color for in-between people who have already seen the light and are not afraid of the dark.

The Gray Knight was not aware that the little fellow favored him. If he'd known this information, it probably wouldn't have meant much to him. The golden era of knighthood, of King Arthur and his Knights of the Round Table, had been over so long that nobody knew for sure if it had ever really happened. People were becoming mildly bored with knights. Knights were merely another group of misguided individuals drawn to an occupation they were hideously ill-suited for, especially if they were wearing armor and it was raining. What the hell, thought the Gray Knight, chivalry was getting a bit rusty as well.

"What's the kid been doin'?" asked the White Knight, who'd drifted back beside him.

"Scribbling in his tablet," said the Gray Knight.

"Just scribbling in his tablet? Just like he's doing now? Doesn't he ever look around to see the scenery?"

"Nope. He's been just like you see him, head down, scribbling in his tablet."

"What do you think he's drawing?" asked the White Knight.

"I'm not going to ask him," said the Gray Knight. "He might look at me with those eyes and turn me into a pillar of fire."

Uncle Floyd did not want to disturb the boy while he was working either, but for a very different reason. He believed that to interrupt an artist at work, whether he was ten years old or not, could hinder the creation of beauty in the world. His son, and he considered him that, was a genius of the first order. The boy would show him his work when he felt it was ready. To stop him in the middle might be distracting him from creating a masterpiece.

Uncle Floyd, however, was not above surreptitiously sneaking a peak at Benjamin's work every once in a while. Now he was startled to see that the lad was busily putting the finishing touches on what appeared to be an inn called the Pregnant Sweetheart. The inn was surrounded by tall fir trees and situated next to a beautiful lake. In the lake were a large number of ducks, swimming and frolicking as the evening fell.

Uncle Floyd peered intently at the road ahead. He looked to his left and to his right. Nowhere could he see a sign of fir trees or a lake, much less the Pregnant Sweetheart. Even the topography of the land seemed different from Benjamin's drawing. Possibly, the child had read about such a place in one of the books he was always reading, thought Uncle Floyd. But that also seemed unlikely. Very unlikely, indeed.

All day the wagon clattered and splattered along the still muddy road until by late afternoon the hot sun had baked everything back to dust again. Up hills and down went the little entourage, stopping only briefly to water and rest the horses. When Benjamin was not busy drawing, he sat very erect in the seat beside his uncle, never turning his head to either side, seemingly scanning the far horizon. What the boy was seeing or what he was looking for, no earthly mind could tell. He just sat there, staring straight ahead, perhaps hypnotized by the hours, perhaps mesmerized by the miles. And yet his mind was traveling faster than the fastest steed could run.

He was seeing Jesus washing his wounds in the lake with all the ducks swimming and flapping their wings in joyous circles all around him. He was seeing his Aunt Joan watching by the little window in the kitchen, waiting for his return. He was seeing the White Knight with his hands all dripping with red blood. Whether he imagined these things, whether he simply saw them in his young, febrile mind, whether they came to him or he came to them, even Benjamin did not know. All he knew was he wanted the world to be good.

Although he could clearly see images of his Aunt Joan missing him, to be truthful, he did not really miss her. He had never in his life missed anyone. He did not know what missing was. Even his interest in the red-bearded Viking was more of an instinctive thing, possibly a scientific inclination, having observed that both their hair was red and the eyes of both were blue. Something had pulled him toward the Viking but now it was gone. Now he was watching the ducks swimming in circles in the lake, round and round in beautiful, perfectly round circles of blue inside his eyes.

CHAPTER SEVEN

The Pregnant Sweetheart

I T WASN'T THAT the boy had no emotions. He had them, all right. He just couldn't quite connect with them in order to express them so others could see. Benjamin was happy and Benjamin was sad, only his moods got all mixed up inside him and resulted in a state of even-mindedness that appeared cold to the conventional eye. Right at the moment, however, he was just a small boy on a seemingly interminable road trip. More than anything else, Benjamin felt tired.

Meanwhile, back on the farm, Aunt Joan was sitting at the little window in her kitchen watching the road, waiting for Benjamin to return. She was well

43

aware that he'd only set out on the journey that very morning, but nonetheless, she found herself already anticipating his arrival back at the farm. She thought with a wry wistfulness of the only time she'd ever really seen the boy laugh. It was a healthy, hearty laugh, just like the fun-loving laughter of other boys his age. Unfortunately, the timing of Benjamin's laughter had proved to be hideously inappropriate. She remembered the episode quite well.

It had been on a freezing morning perhaps four years ago when Benjamin had been six years old. Joan had been returning from the barn where she'd milked the cow. Suddenly, she'd stepped on a frozen puddle and her feet had gone completely out from under her. She went flying and the milk pail went flying and the next thing she knew she'd hit the ground very hard, certain that she'd broken her back. Standing over her and laughing like it was the funniest thing he'd ever seen in his life was Benjamin.

She smiled as she sat in the kitchen thinking about it. After all, she hadn't been hurt. At least not as much hurt as she felt now. How could she have permitted them to take the child so far away?

44

The Christmas Pig

"Time is running out!" shouted King Jonjo, as he strode about his royal chambers in his royal underwear. "Where is this magical boy you promised me?"

"The journey may take a week, your majesty," said Feinberg, pacing along behind the king. "The knights have only been out for four days. Or have the days only been out for four knights?"

"I warn you, Feinberg. No games. Now where are your shoes?"

"I hate to report this, your majesty, but they appear to have run off with your pants."

The king laughed heartily, perhaps in much the same manner as had the small boy seeing his aunt lying flat and still on the cold, hard ground. The truth was that kings rarely if ever got the opportunity to banter with anyone. To properly banter, the humor ball had to go back and forth from one court to the other, which, of course, was impossible when there was only one court and it belonged to the king. Bantering with King Jonjo was second nature to

Feinberg, however. He'd lived on the edge most of his life and he saw no real advantage to his being cautious now. Nonetheless, the thing with the kid was one of the riskiest endeavors he'd ever undertaken. To champion a ten-year-old idiot savant he'd never even met in the hope that the child would please the king, well, this made mere royal bantering look easy. But this was exactly how Feinberg had survived as advisor to the king for all these many years. He knew King Jonjo better than King Jonjo knew himself.

"I want to see the boy!" shouted the king. "I want to look him in the eye!"

"You will, my liege," said Feinberg soothingly, as if speaking to a child and not a king. "Very soon you will."

"What if the boy is an imposter?" persisted King Jonjo. "What if he makes a fool of the court?"

"Never happen," said Feinberg. "This child, your majesty, will become an artist known and appreciated throughout the civilized world. And you, my liege, will be his patron."

"I'm already his patron," hissed the king. "I'm

everybody's patron. This is *my* kingdom, in case you have forgotten."

"Your majesty, the world of art and the world of power are two separate worlds and neither is a re-specter of the other. If you are courageous enough to take this chance, you will have the chance to become king of them both."

"Ahhh," said the king, as he put on his trousers.

●　　●　　●

Darkness was falling as the little caravan plodded along down the dusty road. The miles and the hours had taken their toll upon all of them, although Benjamin looked precisely as he had as they'd pulled out of The Mermaid. The boy felt a little different, however, whether or not he showed it. It is difficult enough to be disconnected from the world. That was how he always felt. Now he was also disconnected from the world he knew. Now, like a great spirit in a new universe, totally unsmudged by life, he knew everything he needed to ride into the unknown. Benjamin had never been afraid of the dark. Ben-

47

jamin had never been afraid of anything. Indeed, he felt at the moment what any little boy would feel, tired.

At last, the party turned off the main road following a sign directing them to lodgings for the night. Soon they noticed fir trees on either side of the road. Then they saw a big lake. Next to the lake was an inn called the Pregnant Sweetheart. The knights took the horses to the stables while Uncle Floyd took the boy to his quarters for the night. The boy was sound asleep as soon as his head hit the pillow. Uncle Floyd quietly took the little drawing pad and headed down to the pub for a pint.

The place was not crowded and he quickly spotted the three knights at a small table by the bar. They motioned for him to join them and this he did, after signaling the barkeep for a pint.

"The young lad's a good traveler," said the White Knight. "Not any trouble at all."

"He's never any trouble," said Uncle Floyd.

"The only trouble he'll have," laughed the Black Knight, "is if his work displeases the king."

"I don't believe that will be a problem," said Uncle

Floyd confidently. "He paints it as he sees it and there's nothing worth painting that Benjamin doesn't see."

"He didn't seem to see much today," offered the Gray Knight. "Head down scribbling all the time or else looking straight ahead at the road."

"We come to see what we want to see," said the old farmer. "What the boy misses isn't worth having."

"He'll have his chance soon enough," said the White Knight. "I figure we're halfway to the court." With that, he ordered another round for the table.

Uncle Floyd bore no ill will toward the three gentlemen from the court. They were, he felt, just doing their jobs. Indeed, he saw their intrusion into his family's life as potentially a great opportunity. It bothered him a bit that his wife did not see it that way, but Joan had always been a worrier. If the lad could successfully complete his commission, his career as an artist would be assured and the farm would be saved. That, to Uncle Floyd, seemed to be worth whatever the risks that might be incurred. He had brought Benjamin's drawing pad down to the pub to peruse himself. Now he decided to share the boy's work with his drinking partners. Let them see the true talents of the young lad currently in their charge.

"My lords," he said, "here is the sketch that Benjamin completed before the noonday sun passed over us in the sky. He had put the sketchbook away entirely many hours before we even so much as turned off the road to this place."

"Mother of God," said the White Knight, in a state of genuine shock.

"It's a perfect representation of this place," said the Black Knight. "And he's never been off the farm?"

"Never," said the farmer.

"He's not only a great artist," exclaimed the Gray Knight. "He's a bloody fortune-teller."

"Art is a strange thing," said Uncle Floyd. "Benjamin has a real opportunity here, I believe. Sometimes it takes a century or more for a great artist to be recognized."

"And who's got the time for that?" said the Black Knight.

"Wait a minute!" shouted the White Knight. "I've

found the flaw in the lad's work. He's drawn ducks all over the lake but there are no ducks. Where are the ducks?"

The barman, who'd been casually listening to the conversation, now came out from around the bar. He took off his apron, walked over to the table, and craned his neck to see the masterpiece in question.

"Where are the ducks?" repeated the White Knight.

"They were here, all right, your lordship," said the barman. "Looked just like this picture. Hundreds of 'em. Then the hunters came and killed most of 'em and the rest never came back. Nary a one."

"Can't blame 'em," said the Black Knight. "When was this bloody massacre when the hunters killed the ducks?"

"Ten years ago, your worship."

"Now, how, in the sacred name of the Lord," said the Gray Knight, "did this young lad know about the ducks?"

"Benjamin appears to know the past quite well," said Uncle Floyd. "He also seems to be spot-on when it comes to relating to the future. His only problem is dealing with the present."

"Join the club," said the Black Knight.

Uncle Floyd stared thoughtfully into his pint. He really didn't know how the boy so accurately portrayed the future and the past. He hadn't a clue as to the source of his wondrous artistic talents. Possibly, only the lad himself knew the answer.

If Benjamin knew, however, he wasn't talking.

CHAPTER EIGHT

The Man on the Bridge

THE LITTLE CARAVAN was halfway through the second day of travel when the highwaymen attacked seemingly out of nowhere. Two of them swept in from the left side of the nearby hedgerow and two more from the back right flank. By the time the White Knight turned around, the Gray Knight had been knocked off his horse and was lying on the ground. One of the highwaymen tried to grab the reins of the horses carrying Uncle Floyd and Benjamin but the White Knight came charging toward him with sword drawn. The White Knight and the highwayman were soon taking broad swipes at each other's heads with gleaming swords as Uncle Floyd endeavored as best he could to protect the young boy from an errant swing of the steel blades.

Throughout this ordeal, Benjamin expressed almost no emotion. This was partly because of the fact that Benjamin always expressed almost no emotion. It was possible that Benjamin had already witnessed the outcome of this event the day before when he'd seen the White Knight with blood on his hands and Jesus with the ducks.

Suddenly, the sounds of muskets being fired could be heard at close range. The Black Knight shot one of the intruders and the man fell from his horse. Another highwayman pulled out his pistol and took aim at the White Knight, who was still locked in battle with the sword-flailing assailant. The shot went wide, hitting the side of the cart, further spooking the horses and causing Benjamin to place his hands over his ears. The child did not perform this action in a hurried or traumatized fashion but rather in a calm, almost robotic manner. The sound of the pistols, evidently, was irritating his ears. This was, indeed, a distraction because, in the midst of the carnage, the boy had begun to start sketching again.

He was drawing the sword fight that was occurring right before his eyes and putting his hands to his ears had caused him to miss the White Knight shoving his sword clear through the gut of his erstwhile opponent. Upon witnessing this, the lad, quite naturally, began sketching again.

These behaviors did not indicate that the young artist was cold or uncaring. It meant merely that he did not express what emotions he felt in a manner that others could see or understand. Some might interpret his attitude as fatalistic to the extreme but this would not necessarily be correct either. A fatalistic attitude would be a rather redundant armament to one who already knew the outcome of any given event. Not that Benjamin could totally predict the future with any more clarity than anyone else. He simply had dreams. He sometimes saw, in waking hours, pictures in his head. He was no different, he felt, from Don Quixote or Joan of Arc, both of whom he'd read about and both of whom he admired, notwithstanding, of course, the fact that one of them, in the purely literal sense, never lived.

Now, as Benjamin looked up briefly from his

sketching, he saw the White Knight extracting his blood-red sword from the body of his adversary and he heard yet another musket shot ring out. He watched as the White Knight's body stiffened rather strangely and his hands went to his heart almost as if he were saying a prayer, which, quite possibly, he was. The White Knight held his blood-covered hands to the sky, and then he dropped to the dust from which all knights are born.

The remaining two highwaymen rode off into the hills. The Gray Knight got up from the ground shaking his head as if to clear the cobwebs and got back on his horse. The White Knight was buried by the side of the road, and a simple wooden cross adorned with his colors was left to commemorate his existence. He had finally met the man on the bridge.

The caravan moved onward toward the court of King Jonjo, with the Black Knight riding on one side and the Gray Knight riding on the other. For his part, Benjamin was currently absorbed in busily, blithely, obliviously sketching in his little art portfolio. Benjamin did not really miss the White Knight. Benjamin had never missed anyone at all.

CHAPTER NINE

A Magical Boy in King Jonjo's Court

MAGICAL BOY! Magical boy!" shouted the king, after downing another hefty swig of absinthe. "Your only effect is to annoy!"

"Now, now, your majesty," said Feinberg. "The couriers have informed the castle that the boy is inside our gates within five or six hours. His name, by the way, is Benjamin."

"Ben! Ben! Ben! Ben!" sang the king. "You're the reason we practice zen."

It would be funny, Feinberg reflected, if it wasn't so pathetic. With all the kingly pursuits that the king could and should be pursuing, he invariably managed to obsess upon matters most trivial. Once, his majesty had spent many months poring over the plans for the new croquet court, which, as things had transpired, was never built. Another time, the king had spent countless days coordinating campaign colors with the White Knight, who, incidentally, according to courier dispatches, had recently been vanquished on the road to the court. Easy come, easy go, thought Feinberg, who was not a great devotee of knights in general. Where were they when you really needed them? And now the king had focused entirely, to the exclusion of all other royal affairs, on the rapid creation of the nativity art for the Christmas mass by a young idiot savant whom Feinberg prayed was more savant than he was idiot. If that were not the case, Feinberg feared, he himself would be rapidly regarded as an idiot. And in the court of King Jonjo, that could mean death or worse.

"Ben-jamin! Ben-jamin!" sang the king, helping himself to another adult portion of absinthe. "When, oh, when, will you begin?"

"Really, your majesty," appealed Feinberg. "When the boy gets here he must rest. Then we must clean him up a bit from his long journey before we can properly present him to the court. After all, your worship, the lad is only ten."

"Ten! Ten! Ten! Ten!" intoned the king, now up and marching around his private quarters. "The bloody childhood's got to end! If indeed the child can't draw," the monarch continued merrily, "I'll cut his body with a saw."

"Your majesty!" cried Feinberg, feigning dismay. Feinberg had become quite adept at feigning dismay over the years. He'd become quite adept at feigning practically everything else as well. That, indeed, was how he'd first gained the confidence of the king. Now, if he could just make it through Christmas Eve with his head still attached to his shoulders. No doubt about it, there was more than just the royal vanity riding on young Benjamin Welch. If the boy were to fail, the entire realm would shudder in the storm of King Jonjo's royal wrath. At the moment, the king was humming to himself what sounded like a little sea chantey.

"If Ben is slow I shall enjoy," sang the king, "having the chance to stab the boy."

"Your majesty!" cried Feinberg, feigning a somewhat subdued state of shock.

One would think a young boy's eyes would pop right out of his head upon hearing the welcoming trumpets and entering a castle gate for the first time in his life. This, of course, was not the case with Benjamin. Nor was he busily sketching the moat, the castle walls, or the many banners fluttering freely in the breeze. He was merely ending the journey much the way he'd started, sitting stock-still in the seat of the wagon next to his Uncle Floyd. Whatever he was thinking, whatever journeys his mind was traveling, belonged to him and him alone. Benjamin was seemingly unimpressed with what he saw. After all, Benjamin knew all there was to know about moats and castle walls. They'd surrounded and protected his mind, heart, and soul since the day he was born.

"So this is the young gentleman," said Feinberg,

extending a hand of welcome, "who's going to make the king very proud."

Benjamin looked at the man's hand as if it were a chafing dish. Feinberg, after a short hesitation, returned the hand to his side.

"And who would this be?" he asked of the farmer, his ingrained unctuous spirit reviving.

"I'm Benjamin's uncle, Floyd Welch," he said, as he shook hands with Feinberg.

"Well, Benjamin's uncle," said Feinberg exuberantly. "Welcome to Eddystone Castle! Let's get the two of you washed up and fed and ready to be presented at the court of King Jonjo first thing in the morning. Several of the king's servants are on hand to extend special care in helping to bathe and clothe our young artist here. A sumptuous feast has been prepared for both of you, as well. We hope you'll enjoy the accommodations."

"There are a few little problems," said Uncle Floyd politely.

"And these few little problems are?" said Feinberg.

"Benjamin will bathe and clothe himself. If the servants will prepare the washtub and lay out his

61

wardrobe, the lad will be fine. They are not to touch him or wash him, or watch him. Is that clear?"

"Very clear, sir," said Feinberg grimly. "Is there more?"

"Yes, sire. This feast you have planned—"

"It is to be a very spectacular affair. The royal chefs have outdone themselves."

"The boy would like oatmeal."

"Oatmeal?"

"Oatmeal. That's all he eats."

"Then oatmeal it is!" said Feinberg with a flourish. "Benjamin will have the finest oatmeal in the kingdom! How does that sound, young man?"

The boy stood still as a rock, his expression changing not a whit, his eyes uncipherable, his soul unknowable. Feinberg observed the child in an attitude of dismay that may not have been entirely feigned. Then he turned back to the boy's uncle.

"Can the boy hear me?" he asked.

"Of course, sire," said the farmer. "He is not deaf."

"Then Benjamin," said Feinberg glowingly, "you will discover in your chambers the finest easel in the kingdom, made of rare koa wood, a gift from the court to you. Also for you, my lad, a beautiful brand-new canvas and all the paints and brushes you can imagine. While you're here at Eddystone Castle, feel free to paint to your heart's content!"

Benjamin showed no reaction whatsoever to this news. Not a muscle in his body twitched, not a flicker could be seen in those odd, robin's-egg-blue eyes.

"So if there's nothing else," said Feinberg, feigning the role of hospitable host, "welcome again to the court of King Jonjo the First. The servants will show you to your quarters. In the morning you shall be presented to the court."

As the old farmer and the strange young child were being shown to their quarters, Feinberg wondered once again if it all was worth it. His job as advisor to the king for many years had necessitated that he sail as close to the truth as he could without sinking the ship. The truth was an iceberg around which no monarch had ever been able to navigate. The truth was he didn't know if this kid could do it. He was weird-looking enough to be an artist. But could he even understand the gravity of a commission from the king? Could he complete the work in time for the Christmas midnight mass? And the most troublesome question of all: What was the art going to look like when this child completed it?

Feinberg had virtually everything riding on this. He himself, having overheard comments in court, had first brought the magical boy's existence to the king. For all he knew the kid's reputation might be bogus. It might also be likely that the kid might be as uncooperative as he was unresponsive.

For once, Feinberg did not have to feign an attitude. Feinberg was worried. Very worried, indeed.

CHAPTER TEN

The King & I

I N THE MORNING, when the servants entered Benjamin's quarters with yet another bowl of oatmeal, they found the bed unslept in, the easel turned to the wall, and the magical boy nowhere to be seen. They quickly alerted Feinberg and then woke the boy's uncle, who'd been sleeping in the next room. An all-points bulletin was put out amongst the royal servants and they scattered all about the castle searching for the wayward lad. Hither and thither scurried the servants but they found no sign of Benjamin.

"I can't understand it," said Uncle Floyd. "He's never done this before."

"He'll never do it again," said Feinberg grimly. "I'm to bring him before the king in one hour's time."

"It's so unlike Benjamin to wander off like this," said Uncle Floyd.

"The king musn't hear of it," Feinberg confided. "He'll think the boy ungrateful."

"Benjamin is very appreciative of the king's commission for the painting. He knows it could help us save the farm."

"How do you know this?" Feinberg pounced. "Did he tell you this?"

"I know Benjamin," said Uncle Floyd.

As the frenzied minutes ticked away, the two men joined the royal servants in the search for the missing boy. In very different ways, and for very different reasons, both the king's advisor and the old farmer were deeply troubled by the boy's disappearance. Uncle Floyd remembered Aunt Joan's dire warnings about removing the boy from the farm and taking him to the court. He could see his wife crying as she waved goodbye. He could hear her scolding him for doing this to Benjamin.

Feinberg was equally unsettled by the whole experience. He had heard the scuttlebutt around the court even before the boy went missing. He had listened as the knights and noblemen and courtiers whispered and sniggered amongst themselves, referring to the affair as "Feinberg's Folly." Now he could hear that phrase ringing in his ears. The boy must be found immediately, he thought.

"The boy could not have left the castle," said Feinberg, with more confidence than he felt. "We'll start at the top and work our way down."

Feinberg was no slouch when it came to divining the future, either. By sheer luck and native instinct, he and the farmer had not searched the perimeter for more than ten minutes when they located the magical boy. He was sound asleep between two turrets, looking for all the world like any other tired ten-year-old. The boy, having no apparent knowledge that the entire royal staff had been furiously searching for him, merely opened his eyes and fixed Feinberg with an eerie blue gaze that cut through his soul like a carving knife. Nevertheless, it was arguable as to which of the two men was most relieved.

"Benjamin!" said Uncle Floyd. "Thank God you're all right."

"There you are, my lad!" said Feinberg, with as much joviality as he'd ever felt in his life. "We must not keep the king waiting now, must we?"

The boy looked disreputable, almost as if he'd slept in his clothes, which, of course, he had. It would take a good half hour to get him clean enough to present to the king, thought Feinberg. Maybe longer because the servants could not wash him or even supervise the exercise. Feinberg would have to rely upon the old peasant to make the lad presentable. This being the case, he did his best to hustle both of them back to the boy's quarters as quickly as he could.

Like most ten-year-olds, Benjamin did not especially like to bathe. Interestingly enough, he did not dislike Feinberg. The cold gaze that had so unnerved the court advisor actually contained no degree of malice whatsoever. It was, instead, the mirror opposite of what one observed in the practiced, cunning, duplicitous gaze of Feinberg himself, and most other humans for that matter. It was the open, trusting unvarnished gaze of a babe, a Christ on the cross, or a ten-year-old magical boy who didn't know how to miss anyone, but wondered vaguely how his Aunt Joan was doing back on the farm. Feinberg had never seen a person look at him before with a countenance containing no bullshit whatsoever. Pure intellect, pure truth, pure humanity, are qualities that people are not very adept at dealing with, Feinberg being no exception. Feinberg was only different in that he did not show his feelings. In this respect, he was more similar to the boy than he ever could have imagined.

Back in the boy's room, it was determined that the lad would bathe himself in his uncle's quarters whilst the servants would provide an appropriate wardrobe for the lad to meet the king. As these royal ablutions were taking place, Feinberg paced back and forth in Benjamin's empty suite. A strange boy, he reflected, to wander at night through a strange castle to fall asleep in its parapets.

Feinberg noticed the easel in its new position turned facing the wall. He walked over to it and turned it around so he could see the canvas. It was only then that true terror struck deep into his heart. It had not crossed his mind that the magical boy might, indeed, have a sense of humor. He hadn't figured into the equation the possibility that this odd little genius or idiot savant or whatever the hell he was might be capable of something called ten-year-old mischief.

The painting on the canvas, if one wished to call it that, depicted three stick figures, possibly standing in front of what could be construed as the castle. They might conceivably have represented the boy, the uncle, and Feinberg himself, although they were so ill-fashioned and drawn so crudely it was virtually impossible to determine whom they were actually intended to represent. The painting, indeed, thought Feinberg, looked very much like the work of—well—a ten-year-old.

"If there's a God in heaven," said Feinberg to himself, "the king will never see this."

The trumpets sounded. Benjamin Welch and Floyd Welch were announced to the court of King Jonjo the First and marched in across the blood-red carpet with Feinberg right behind them. On either side of the boy and his uncle, the court was crowded with curious noblemen, knights, and various and sundry members of the royal court all decked out in finery fitting for the occasion. Benjamin entered rather awkwardly, his hands still tightly clapped over his ears. He did not like the sound of trumpets.

"Your royal highness," said Feinberg reverentially. "I have the unique pleasure and honor of introducing to your majesty one of the greatest young undiscovered talents in the kingdom. May I present Benjamin Welch and his uncle, Floyd Welch."

The trumpets sounded again. Uncle Floyd bowed deeply to the king, but Benjamin, who'd only moments earlier placed his hands down by his sides, now covered his ears once again, standing almost blasphemously erect in front of the king, and fixing him with his patented robin's-egg-blue stare. Benjamin liked the sparkle on King Jonjo's crown. It reminded him of snowflakes on the windowsill.

"Welcome to Eddystone Castle, young Benjamin," said the king, "and welcome to my court."

In response, Benjamin brought his hands down

71

slowly to his sides and remained standing mute as a statue before the king. This produced a mild titter amongst some of the courtiers, which King Jonjo silenced immediately by raising his scepter approximately a quarter of an inch.

"Your majesty," interjected Feinberg, "the boy does not speak."

"Very wise," said the king. "If only the rest of my subjects could follow his lead."

The silent court grew silenter still. The curious contented themselves with gawking at the little boy, obviously uncomfortable in his courtly apparel, and his uncle, for whom no proper wardrobe had been prepared, standing in the midst of all the royal finery in the overalls and boots of a simple farmer.

"Your majesty," said Feinberg, "the boy can hear you well and understands implicitly what you say. May I suggest your highness explain to Benjamin what is required of him and direct any questions to his uncle or to myself."

"Very well," said the king. "Benjamin, it has long been my policy to treat children like adults and adults like children. In other words, I shall not patronize or beat around the bush with you because of your young years. Do you understand me, lad?"

The boy looked at the king as if he were watching the rear end of a horse as it flicked its tail. He did not so much as nod or blink an eye. King Jonjo continued undeterred.

"Before I give you your instructions, there is another matter I wish to address. It has been brought to my attention by persons close to the court that through your art you are able to predict the future. Is it true, my lad?"

Benjamin, of course, said nothing. The king matched him stare for stare. The court held its collective breath to see which of the two would first blink. At last, Feinberg jumped in between them, in a gallant effort to save the pride of the king.

"Your majesty has inquired whether or not this young child can predict the future," he said. "Perhaps the question could be best answered by the lad's uncle."

"Very well," said the king, turning slightly on his royal throne toward Uncle Floyd. "Can this lad of yours, sir, predict the future?"

"Sometimes he can, your majesty," he said, with a little bow, "and sometimes he can't."

"What good is that?" shouted the king.

The assembled members of the court voiced their approval of the sentiment, nodding their heads and shouting, "Hear! Hear!" Again Feinberg, sensing the situation was spinning out of control, insinuated himself into the proceedings.

"Your worship," he said, "perhaps we are getting a bit far afield from our purposes here today. Whether or not the boy can speak, whether or not he can predict the future, whether or not, indeed, he is truly a magical boy, these matters can be pursued at our leisure. We stand here less than two fortnights away from the traditional royal Christmas midnight mass, an event of great gravity and significance not only to the court but to all the subjects of the realm. The question is, can the child standing mutely before your majesty and the court create a work of art depicting the traditional nativity scene, the birth of our Savior, that shall engender joy and inspiration to all the people of the kingdom? And can he do it very quickly?"

The Christmas Pig

King Jonjo paused to puff on his pipe and to absorb the words of the royal advisor. To the members of the court it seemed unclear if the odd young lad standing in front of him had indeed heard or understood anything that had transpired. Who could safely place such an august assignment in the hands of such a boy? Was it wise for the king to grant a royal commission to one so young, so inscrutable, and so unknown to the court? Only King Jonjo could make this fateful decision from which the entire kingdom might well reap a bitter harvest.

The king seemed to be taking his time. The boy might as well have been made out of marble. The court whispered and twittered with doubt and uncertainty. Feinberg privately feared that this time he might have overstepped himself. He'd made a career out of betting on the long shot and watching it come through. This time, however, he wasn't so sure. Nevertheless, his future was irretrievably intertwined with the success of this peculiar endeavor. He was the one in the first place who'd introduced the king to the notion of the magical boy. He was the one who'd seduced the king into believing in the lad's prowess. Sometimes, thought Feinberg, you've just got to play it as it lays.

"Benjamin Welch," the king intoned in a deep, stern voice, almost as if he were pronouncing a death sentence, "I hereby entrust you with the royal task of delivering a finished and satisfactory piece of art before midnight on the Eve of December 25, the birthday of our Lord. The art must be pleasing to the eyes of the king. Mr. Floyd Welch?"

"Yes, your majesty," said Uncle Floyd, stepping forward and bowing once again.

"Does this young man, Benjamin Welch, understand the terms of the royal commission I am about to entrust to him? Does he fully realize that, if completed successfully, it will surely bring him great riches? But if he fails to deliver the work of art in timely fashion, or if his creation displeases the royal court, I will take it not only as an insult to my royal throne but also as an offense to the child who was born on that day."

"He understands, your majesty," said the farmer in a clear voice.

"If Benjamin Welch completes the royal commis-

76

sion successfully, the entire kingdom shall rejoice!" said the king. The gathered court greeted this pronouncement with an encouraging display of light applause. Feinberg allowed himself to beam beatifically upon Benjamin. Benjamin, of course, showed no reaction whatsoever to the proceedings.

"If he fails," said the king, "those responsible shall suffer the fate of a thousand scoundrels." The assembled court shuddered as one at the dark thought. Feinberg's face became suddenly almost as void of emotion as Benjamin's.

"It shall be done," said King Jonjo, pointing his royal scepter directly at Benjamin.

The boy did not flinch. He liked the royal scepter. It looked like it was covered with fireflies.

CHAPTER ELEVEN

Uncle and Son

EARLY THE NEXT MORNING the little wagon with its entourage departed from the gates of Eddystone Castle. There were no trumpets this time, for which Benjamin was eternally grateful, though, of course, he didn't show it. The caravan consisted of different personnel for the return trip. Instead of the White, Black, and Gray Knights, there was the Blue Knight and the Green Knight and a nobleman whose title was Sir Myers of Keswick. Feinberg had vouchsafed to Uncle Floyd prior to departure that Sir Myers was one of the highest-ranking noblemen in the realm. This was a good sign, Feinberg had stated, because it indicated that the king had confidence in the boy's abilities. Uncle

Floyd had confidence in the boy as well. He just wasn't sure if any artist on earth, much less a child, could create a masterpiece in three weeks' time.

Feinberg, in spite of the ebullient send-off he'd given to Benjamin and his uncle, had his doubts as well. He'd personally destroyed the crude, offending, stick-figure canvas the boy had left in his quarters. He did not want even a servant to see the monstrous thing. Feinberg had had a night to sleep on it and now he prayed that it was a childish prank and did not represent the high-water mark of the lad's abilities. The boy's uncle had shown Feinberg an excellent drawing of an inn called the Pregnant Sweetheart complete with ducks on a lake that he purported to be the work of the child. He'd also made the rather outlandish assertion that the boy had drawn it many miles before he'd, indeed, arrived within sight of the place.

The two surviving knights—the White and Black—no, no, it was the *Gray* and the Black, the White Knight had been vanquished. Feinberg never could keep the knights straight. Anyway, several of them had reported witnessing the boy scribbling in his drawing pad along the journey but that alone did not totally corroborate that the Pregnant Sweetheart was his work. Regrettably, Feinberg had no firsthand evidence that the boy had ever painted anything of merit. Feinberg was going by his gut and just at the moment his gut was upset.

Uncle Floyd had packed the paints and brushes and the new canvas into the wagon and thanked Feinberg profusely. The old farmer was tired of traveling and tired of the court and he knew that Benjamin was, too. If they could just get back to the farm without more death and destruction the boy could rest up and then do a masterful job of fulfilling the trust the king had placed in him. And how happy his wife would be, thought Uncle Floyd, to see the two of them arriving safely home.

"You should be very proud of your nephew," said Sir Myers of Keswick, riding alongside the wagon. "I believe he's the youngest person in my memory to ever receive a royal commission from the king."

"I am proud of him," said Uncle Floyd to the kind nobleman. "He's not really my nephew, though. He's not really even my son. He's more than a son."

"More than a son?" said Sir Myers. "That's a wonderful thing to be."

Once Sir Myers of Keswick rode on up ahead a bit, Uncle Floyd found an old cigar in his overalls, inspected it thoroughly, and lit it up. He settled back in the seat, next to but not quite touching Benjamin. Since the child had been three or four years old, the farmer had never remembered having any physical contact with the boy. He had always not quite touched him. That was how Benjamin wanted it to be and that was how it was. And yet it could not be said that he was a cold child. He was warm and loving if you knew how to read him. The boy, in fact, was an open book. Now Uncle Floyd found himself talking to Benjamin at the same time as he was thinking to himself.

"You are more than a son, Benjamin," he said. "Like your Aunt Joan says, you are a gift from heaven to both of us. We were sent here to look after you and you were sent here to look after us. It is your talent, Benjamin, yours and yours alone, that may well serve to get us out of debt and save the farm. I never intended it to be that way. I intended to take care of you but now it seems that you are the breadwinner in the family. You are in a position to take care of us."

If the boy heard the old man, it was impossible to know. He looked straight ahead as the wagon jolted along the dusty, rutted road in the brittle sunlight of a chill December. Though the boy did not respond, had never responded as most boys do, Uncle Floyd was aware of feeling something good and decent emanating from the heart of the child. Something was there. Something was being communicated. Something.

"I wish we could have done better for you, son," he said. "More important than anything we've ever done is the challenge before you now. If your work pleases the king, you will soon be hailed as the great artist that your Aunt Joan and I already know you are. The world will know your talents, Benjamin. The world."

The red-haired boy heard every word his uncle had said. Every syllable had been processed somewhere deep in his soul. He liked the way the wagon rocked gently and ever so often slightly jolted him. He did not like the trumpets.

"We love you very much, son," his uncle was saying. "We love you more than any king's commission. And so we always shall."

Angels were whispering to Benjamin. Or was it merely the murmuring of the wind?

●   ●   ●

When the royal entourage finally rolled into the little hamlet of Long Lama, it was three days later. Almost as if he'd sensed their arrival, the Viking was standing out in front of The Mermaid scouring the road. It would be difficult to assess what the boy felt when he saw the Viking. Certainly no joyful emotion leapt across his countenance. In fact, his expression, his demeanor, registered virtually no change at all. Yet the Viking knew. The Viking was a sailor who loved the sea.

The little group stopped briefly at The Mermaid. Uncle Floyd conferred with Sir Myers and the two decided that a rest might be in order, still allowing time to reach the farm before dark. While the horses were being attended to and the other travelers hav-

ing lunch, the farmer went out to the wagon and re-
trieved the drawing pad that the Viking had given to
Benjamin. He brought it back inside the pub and
handed it to the big man.

"Benjamin wanted you to see this," he said.

"Aye," said the Viking, gazing at the child's drawing. "The ol' Sweetheart. There's beauty."

"Have you stayed there before?" asked Uncle
Floyd.

"Let's just say," said the Viking, "I've seen the
ducks."

●   ●   ●

It was getting toward dusk by the time they reached
the little wooden bridge between the town and the
farm. Sir Myers of Keswick crossed it first and noticed an old man working the fields with a scythe. Sir
Myers waved to the old man and the man waved
back but his eyes were fixed upon the small redheaded boy seated in the front of the wagon. Benjamin looked briefly at the man, then returned to
busily drawing on his sketchpad.

Aunt Joan was overjoyed to see the wagon with its royal escort rolling onto the farm. She rushed out into the front yard of the old farmhouse and embraced Uncle Floyd. Benjamin walked up to her, handed her the sketchbook, and continued his way into the house. He had almost hugged her this time, she felt. She had almost run her fingers through his hair.

She opened the sketchbook later that evening after the king's men had gone and Benjamin was asleep. By lantern light she gazed with admiration at the child's depiction of the Pregnant Sweetheart. Then she turned the page and saw a drawing of a desolate shoreline. A lighthouse rose from the sea, its light shining evanescently over the waves. In the near distance, a red-haired little boy and an older woman wearing an apron were walking hand in hand on the beach.

CHAPTER TWELVE

A Conversation in a Dream

VERY CHILD AT ONE time or another hears the conversations of adults as the child is falling asleep. The adults often say things they normally would not say if the child were around. Benjamin did not like to eavesdrop but the condition with which he was afflicted had made his auditory abilities exceedingly keen. That was one reason he hadn't liked the trumpets.

The walls of the old farmhouse, as well, were of very thin construction and his room was located right next door to that of his uncle and aunt. Thus, it was virtually impossible for him not to hear their conversations at night. While he felt bad about the eavesdropping part, it made him feel good and comfortable to hear their voices softly speaking to each other in the darkness of the world. To Benjamin it sounded like the murmuring of the wheat in the field, the waves in the ocean, the stars swirling around in the sky, and the angels on his pillow.

"And what if Benjamin doesn't understand this royal commission that's been thrust upon him?" said Aunt Joan, in a voice louder than usual.

"He understands," said Uncle Floyd. "You of all people know that he understands things well beyond his years."

"And what if the child—he *is* still a child—can't finish the painting before the deadline of Christmas Eve? That's less than three weeks from now."

"He'll finish."

The murmuring ceased for a moment. In the ensuing silence, the boy heard the unhappiness and uncertainty of his uncle and aunt. He wanted them to be happy, whatever that was. The books he had read had not explained the definition of happiness nor how it could be obtained. At the moment he wasn't sure if he was dreaming or awake and all he wanted was to listen to Uncle Floyd and Aunt Joan murmuring again.

"The court has provided a nice new canvas, and paints and brushes of the finest quality," Uncle Floyd was saying. "Benjamin doesn't sleep much and he can work in his little studio in the barn—"

"It gets cold at night in the barn."

"He'll wrap a quilt around himself. The point is he's got all the animals right there in the barn to use for subjects as he paints the babe in the manger."

"That's true. I just worry about all this deadline business putting too much pressure on the child. He *is* only ten."

"But Benjamin's a veteran soul. He's wise beyond anything he's read in books. He knows how important this could be for us all."

"Are you *sure* he knows?"

"Sure I'm sure. I told him. The king told him. Besides, he just knows."

"I hope you're right, Floyd. For all of our sakes."

"Don't fret yourself, darling."

Benjamin was dreaming now but, in truth, it was not that different from his waking state. His life was a dream into which ripples of reality occasionally intruded. These he always filed away for possible use in a future that only he could see. It did not trouble him that he did not speak, he did not touch, he would only let himself love in the abstract. He was not alone in his aloneness. Many people were very similar to him only they didn't realize it. There were many others who had nothing to say, yet they shouted that nothing to the world. Benjamin knew he had much to say. He just couldn't say it. He couldn't express how he felt except through his art. He would've liked things to be different but they weren't. He was different.

Just now he was tired. He was tired of being Benjamin. He was tired of being a dreamer who never sleeps. He was tired and needed rest but he knew that time was short and most important of all, he could see the finished canvas. All his life he had woken from dreams and still been dreaming. His Aunt Joan had been right. He could not love. He was love. He was a ten-year-old boy but he was also an artist.

He got up and dressed, wrapped a quilt around himself, and walked to the barn. Thus it was that the final adventure began.

CHAPTER THIRTEEN

The Horse

HIS AUNT JOAN had been right, thought Benjamin. The old barn *was* cold and drafty. Even under the quilt, Benjamin shivered. But it was a good shiver. It was the shiver of the artist preparing to pour his passion into his work, to infuse a blank canvas with the colors of his soul. He lit the candles in the lanterns on either side of the easel, causing dark shadows to dance around the barn. This was decidedly not the perfect "studio" in which an artist might choose to work, but it suited Benjamin just fine. After all, he'd already seen the finished canvas in his mind. All that remained was to merely paint it. This, of course, was easier said than done. It was the devil that had haunted the true artist down through eternity. How to transfer the vision from the spiritual studio of the artist's mind to the actual canvas without losing or gaining or changing or explaining? This was the hard part because, indeed, it was so simple.

Benjamin's mind, however, was uniquely up to the task at hand. He did not waste his time with frivolous conversation or extraneous emotion. The boy had a warm heart but his mind was like that cold, spartan attic from which has forever emanated the great art of mankind.

"A horse! A horse! My kingdom for a horse!" was what the child was thinking. He was, of course, well read in the classics. Also the horse, who was called Jezebel, happened to be the nearest animal to his easel.

Jezebel, indubitably, was not the perfect subject an artist would wish to sit for a painting commissioned by a king. She was old, swaybacked, so thin that her ribs were clearly discernible, and of an off-white color that might best be described as pale. This appealed to the boy, nevertheless, because she reminded him of Don Quixote's horse, Rocinante. Don Quixote was the only person who thought that Rocinante was young and beautiful and noble. "I see a pale horse," Don Quixote had opined on his deathbed. The man had never lived, of course, but Benjamin did not know this. He dealt equally well in the casinos of fiction and nonfiction; he had no use for reality.

Thus it was that old, flea-bitten, battle-scarred Jezebel became the most beautiful horse in the world. And this was accomplished largely because Benjamin was beautiful.

He was in the midst of painting the old horse in the flickering candlelight when he heard a voice which he at first thought was in his head. No, it was not in his head. It was a woman's voice, a young woman's voice. It was coming from somewhere nearby in the dark shadows of the old barn.

"I'd say old Jezebel never looked so good," said the voice.

Perhaps it was an angel, thought Benjamin. He looked around but there was no one in the barn. He went back to painting the horse.

"It really is quite excellent work, Benjamin," said the voice.

A normal ten-year-old, even someone much older, would've probably flown out of the barn like a bat out of hell. But not Benjamin. He had heard voices and sounds his whole life, some having been attached to things and people and some had not. Nevertheless, it did unnerve the boy quite enough to pick up one of the lanterns and walk toward the direction from whence he'd heard the young woman's voice.

He took a few more tentative steps, and shone the lantern around. All he saw was the sleeping brown dog and the bright-eyed runty little brown and white pig. He turned around, walked back to his old easel and chair, replaced the lantern on the easel, and picked up his brush.

"Can you speak, Benjamin?" asked the voice, clear and soft in the winter night.

A normal child alone in the barn would have dropped the brush and run for his life. But not Benjamin. He was a little afraid. But he was more curious.

As he watched in disbelief, the little brown and white pig stepped forward into the circle of light.

The pig gazed admiringly at the canvas, then looked directly at Benjamin, the admiration still in her eyes.

"My name is Valerie," she said.

Though Benjamin had never associated with people much and had no involvement with children his age as friends, he knew instinctively that he was different. Nonetheless, he reflected, he wasn't *this* different. He'd never read or heard about a pig who could speak. It just wasn't done. Yet here, right before his own eyes and ears was a pig addressing him by name, speaking to him in a voice more sweet and comforting than the nighttime murmurings of Uncle Floyd and Aunt Joan. And she'd said her name was Valerie.

"Can you speak, Benjamin?" she asked again.

They looked at each other across thousands of years of evolution and ignorance, of love and hate, of life and death. It was not a dream. It was not a fairy tale. It was only what it was.

"Can you?" she asked.

"Yes," he said.

That was how it had all started, and whether the boy or the pig knew it or not, it was to be the beginning of a beautiful friendship. In the morning, the boy woke up in his bed and walked over to the window. He looked down into the barnyard and there was Valerie. He rushed down the stairs and ran out into the bright morning sunlight of the barnyard. The animals were milling about in the chilly early hours of the day. Valerie was there, too. But so was Will Wallace, the farmhand. And Uncle Floyd was close by chopping wood. Benjamin looked at Valerie, but she did not return his gaze. Now she was what she'd always been, it seemed. A pig in the barnyard. Benjamin went back into the house where his Aunt Joan was preparing his oatmeal for breakfast.

That afternoon Benjamin spent his time reading in his room. This was not unusual for the boy. Like many great artists, the boy did his best work late at night. His uncle and aunt were well aware of his proclivity for nocturnal painting and had no problem with it. Nor did they like to in any way intrude upon a work in progress. And this, of course, was the most important work in progress the lad had ever tackled.

The Christmas Pig

This night Benjamin was happy to note that Jezebel was cooperating. The night before she'd refused to sit patiently for the painting, moving around repeatedly inside the barn and finally retreating into her stall and refusing to come out again. Tonight she was enjoying a bucket of oats and being the perfect model. Benjamin was making good progress when he heard a familiar voice from the nearby darkness.

"Sorry I couldn't talk to you this morning," said Valerie. "Will was there. And your Uncle Floyd. It wouldn't feel right for them to know. Ours, it seems, dear Benjamin, is a friendship that cannot speak its name."

"How did you know my name was Benjamin?" asked the boy, a bit warily, as he continued to paint the horse.

"I get around a bit," she said. "I've heard lots of conversations in the barnyard. Just because I'm a pig doesn't mean I can't hear."

"I'm sorry," said Benjamin. "I didn't mean to insult you. People are always asking about me, too. They're always saying, 'Can the lad hear me?' "

"That's because you don't talk," said Valerie.

"Just because I don't talk," said Benjamin, "doesn't mean I can't hear."

"You're making my argument for me, dear Benjamin. Anyway, what does it matter what most people think. It's like what your Aunt Joan says to you, 'You listen with your heart, dear Benjamin.'"

"How do you know what my Aunt Joan says to me?"

"I listen with my heart."

By the time the horse was at last finished, Benjamin had carried on with Valerie the longest and the only conversation of his life. It felt liberating and wonderful and natural, almost like his own heart was talking to his mind.

"It's almost dawn," said Valerie. "You'd better get some rest."

"Will I see you tomorrow night?"

"Of course you will. Good night, dear Benjamin."

"Good night, dear Valerie."

CHAPTER FOURTEEN

The Cow

NELL WAS A VERY THIN, nondescript, brown cow who had definitely seen greener pastures. Like Jezebel the horse, however, Nell was all Benjamin had to work with. Right now she was standing outside her stall eating some hay and the artist was beginning to place her in the portrait. As the boy started to sketch Nell, he found himself wondering when Valerie would make her appearance. All day he'd been looking forward to seeing her. Not just seeing her, *talking* to her.

"Dear Benjamin," she said, walking into the circle of light surrounding the easel. "I've missed you, dear Benjamin."

"I've been thinking of you as well," said the boy, with one eye on the canvas and one eye on the pig.

"But you didn't miss me, did you? You've never missed anybody, have you, Benjamin dear?"

"I guess not."

"Cheer up! You will."

"I hope not," said the boy, continuing to sketch the cow.

"I don't mean to be nosy," said Valerie, as she walked around to the other side of the easel. "But what's this all *for?* Is it for the king? I know you went to meet the king, I saw the knights here on the farm coming to take you away and bring you back. Come on. Stop painting for a minute, Benjamin dear. Tell me what it's all about. A girl gets curious sometimes."

Benjamin put down his brush and turned toward Valerie. Somehow it did not seem so unusual anymore to be carrying on a conversation with a pig. Even the fact that he was having a conversation in the first place no longer seemed so strange.

"Well, it's like this, Valerie," he said, in his charming if somewhat precocious manner. "Believe it or not, the king has given me a royal commission to paint a portrait of the manger scene, the birth of Christ, to be unveiled at the close of the Christmas Eve midnight mass. All the court and the towns-people will gather for the mass and the unveiling at Eddystone Castle. That gives me about two and a half weeks to finish the whole painting, allowing for time to have it delivered to the castle."

It was the most he'd said to anybody ever about anything. Valerie looked duly impressed. She came over a little closer to his chair.

"I don't mean to be nosy," she said again, "but you're a really talented kid and you're busting your hump to finish this project on time. What's the king paying you for all this work?"

"I'm not sure. But according to Uncle Floyd, it's enough to just possibly keep the farm from being taken away from us."

"That would be terrible, dear Benjamin. This place is my home."

"I wish I had a home."

"You do, darling. It's your home, too."

"But I never thought of it as a home."

"Benjamin. Dear Benjamin. You've never believed you had a home. You've never missed anyone. It seems so sad."

"I've never been sad, either."

That night, as Benjamin painted Nell, he continued talking to the pig as he painted. He told Valerie things that he'd never told anyone before. That wasn't terribly surprising, of course, because he'd never told anyone anything before. Nevertheless, he kept talking. And Valerie seemed to be quite appreciative. She was, he thought, an excellent conversationalist.

"You see, Benjamin dear," she'd said at one point late in the night, "pigs do not think of themselves as pigs. And you do not see us that way either. Maybe that's one reason why we get along so well."

"Maybe," said Benjamin.

They talked long into the night and Benjamin found, to his pleasant surprise, that Valerie was not a distraction to his work at all. Not only was she a supportive voice but she proved to occasionally be a pretty fair art critic as well. Like most great artists, he didn't really believe he was a great artist. Also like most great artists, he preferred to paint alone. That, of course, was before he'd met Valerie.

"Now that's what I call talent!" said Valerie. "Making Nell the cow look like she's interested in something."

"Most people think I'm not interested in anything either. I know how it feels."

"Ah, but I know different, Benjamin dear. To be a great artist you have to be interested in everything and everybody. You have to be naturally curious. You have to listen with your heart. You have all those qualities, dear Benjamin. That's how I know you're a great artist."

"Thank you, Valerie."

"Of course, I have those same qualities as well. I just can't hold a brush in my hoof."

"You're more than a great artist, Valerie. You're a great pig."

"Well, thank you, Benjamin dear. I think you meant that as a compliment."

"Of course I did, Valerie. I would never insult you."

"No one should ever be insulted by the truth, dear Benjamin."

A great, closed door in Benjamin's life seemed to be opening up for him. A week ago he had no friends and was all alone in the world. Now he was painting a royal commission from the king and talking to his new best friend. Why should it matter that Valerie was a pig? He loved just sitting in the quiet darkness of the barn and painting and chatting with her. He liked the words they said. He liked the way their voices sounded, starting small, then booming around the big old barn. He couldn't decide if it was stranger to hear her voice or his own.

"Valerie, do you think the other animals can speak?"

"They never said a word to me."

"Do you think other pigs can speak?"

"Don't know. Never met one."

"I wonder."

"What's important, dear Benjamin, is that you and I can speak to each other."

Benjamin put the final touches on Nell the cow and Valerie nodded her head several times in thoughtful approval. Benjamin had been careful to leave plenty of blank canvas to fill in the other animals, the three wise men, and, of course, Jesus, Joseph, and Mary. It was easy to paint a bad manger scene, Benjamin thought. To paint a really good one took not only talent but time. God had given him the talent, Benjamin figured, but apparently, He'd neglected to give him the time.

"Who's next?" asked Valerie.

"Who's next for what?"

"For the painting, dear Benjamin. The horse and the cow are beautiful, but who's next? Is it the lamb? Is it the rooster? Is it me?"

Now, for the first time in his life, Benjamin realized that friendship, along with its comforts and joys, also has its burdens and responsibilities. Both the king and his uncle had made it very clear to him that the painting must be very traditional, historically correct, and biblically accurate. In all the religious literature he'd ever read, there'd been no account of Jesus' people tending pigs. The Old Testa-

105

ment, he knew, forbade eating pork. How in the world, he wondered, could he ever explain this to such a trusting and sensitive friend as Valerie? He'd have to think of how to most gently break the news to her. It was the truth, wasn't it? She'd said herself that no one should ever be insulted by the truth. But there were still two weeks until the deadline. No reason to upset her now. He'd explain it to her later.

"I think I'll paint the lamb next," he said at last.

"No worries, dear Benjamin," she said. "I can wait."

CHAPTER FIFTEEN

The Lamb

THE HARDEST PART about being an artist, thought Benjamin the following morning, was not drawing a horse or a cow. The hardest part was being true to yourself. Benjamin, for the first time, felt a new sensation. He felt a little sad. He didn't cry, of course. He'd never cried in his life. He was just a little sad that his new friend, with whom he so enjoyed conversing and being with, appeared to want so badly to be included in the painting. He wasn't excluding her, he told himself; the ancient Hebrews were excluding her.

He also knew that one false note in a work of art could ruin everything. In this case, it could have the effect of the king retracting the promised commission and the family farm being lost. Even if he didn't think of it as home, Valerie did. What would become of her if the farm were to be taken away? Having heard the vengeful pronouncements by the king, he did not look forward to feeling his royal wrath. If he were to include Valerie in the manger scene, he would probably never work in the kingdom again.

After he'd eaten his oatmeal, he felt a bit better about things. Maybe Valerie would understand after all. Yet, somehow it didn't seem quite fair. Of all the animals in the barnyard, she was the only one he really cared about. And yet all of them would probably end up in the painting except her. He scoured the Old Testament in a feverish effort to find something nice someone had said about pigs, but there was nothing. Nothing at all.

After dark, he walked purposefully into the dusky old barn, lit the lanterns, settled himself into his chair, and reexamined the horse and the cow on the canvas. He was a modest young man but even to his highly critical eyes they looked good. Now where was that little lamb hiding? He took one of the lanterns and began poking around the barn.

"Looking for a lost lamb?" said a friendly, familiar voice. "That could be anybody, dear Benjamin."

"Hey, Valerie," said Benjamin. "It so happens that I am looking for that lost lamb. He's probably asleep."

"Most normal people are, Benjamin dear. But who wants to be normal."

"I quite agree," he said.

"If we were normal," said Valerie, sidling out into the circle of light, "we wouldn't be talking like this. And you wouldn't be painting such a beautiful masterpiece."

"You really think the painting could be a masterpiece?"

"Benjamin, it *will* be a masterpiece. You are a genius, Benjamin dear! How could it be anything other than a masterpiece if it's painted by your fine and talented hand?"

"That's so nice of you to tell me that, Valerie," said the boy, practically blushing.

"I've never told anyone that before," said Valerie.

Benjamin found the lamb asleep in the hay. He set down the lantern and gently carried the little fellow to a location closer to the light. Soon the artist was back at his easel and his favorite art critic was standing beside him watching him work.

"His fleece is definitely not white as snow," Valerie observed.

"It will be when I get through," said Benjamin.

Sure enough, not only was the painted lamb an almost incandescent white, but his eyes, which looked slightly dull and glazed, had also been rendered quite differently on the canvas. Benjamin had duly provided the painted lamb with a suitably adoring gaze.

"You're not just a genius," said Valerie, shaking her head slowly from side to side. "You're a miracle worker."

"Valerie, you're too kind."

"Don't think I'm trying to flatter you, Benjamin, because I'm not. I'm merely stating that your work thus far is quite remarkable. Far from sanitizing these animals or covering up their faults, you've brought out the best in them. You've transformed them with an artist's eye and a Christian heart into how God intended them to be."

"Valerie, I don't think I could get through these long nights without your help and encouragement. You're the best friend I've ever had."

"Good," said the pig. "Then remember, when you paint me, my left profile is my best."

"I'll remember," said Benjamin, as he put away his paints.

"So tomorrow it's my turn?" asked Valerie hopefully.

"We'll see," said Benjamin.

CHAPTER SIXTEEN

The Rooster

THE FOLLOWING NIGHT things finally came to a head. Perhaps all the nocturnal work had put a strain on both of them. The dreaded deadline had been foremost in Benjamin's mind but in Valerie's heart there had begun to form a definite feeling that she was being left out. Indeed, the boy felt sad to see her preening herself in the lantern light. She was a very beautiful pig, Benjamin had to admit. And he told her so. But the knife went in deeper and deeper when she saw that he was painting the rooster. At last, Valerie could no longer restrain her true feelings.

"I can't believe you'd do this, Benjamin," she said,

in a voice filled with hurt. "Picking that scraggly, annoying rooster over me."

The rooster's name was Hitchcock and he had to be painted. Time, Benjamin well knew, was running out. Nonetheless, the boy set down his brush. Hitchcock remained where he was, asleep on a rafter. At least he wasn't going anywhere.

"Valerie," said Benjamin, in a voice he'd intended to sound grown-up but had come out seemingly tinged with guilt. "Valerie, you're my friend. You're the last pig in the world I'd want to hurt. The last person, too."

But Valerie had already gone back to the pigpen and Benjamin could only hear muffled snuffling noises in the darkness. Benjamin pulled the quilt around him in the cold night, grabbed a lantern, and headed in the direction of the sound. At first, he could not quite identify the rather subdued snuffling noises. He had, of course, never heard a pig cry.

In the lives of all pigs and all ten-year-old boys, there comes a day of reckoning, even if that day is in the middle of the night. As gently as possible, in his innate analytical fashion, the boy with the unvarnished eyes told his friend the unvarnished truth. Placing the lantern on the railing, he leaned against the pigsty and spoke softly but clearly.

"The painting the king has commissioned me to create must be a traditional nativity scene, artistically excellent, historically correct, and biblically accurate down to the last brushstroke. The painting is to be unveiled after the midnight mass at Eddystone Castle in the presence of King Jonjo, the entire royal court, the priests, and all the townspeople. If I were to include you in the painting, they would all be horrified and the king would very likely retract his commission and the painting would be considered a failure and we would lose the farm and you and I would have no place to live."

"But, dear Benjamin, it's so unfair. Why can't a pig be in the manger scene with all the other animals?"

"Because the Ancient Hebrews considered the pig to be unclean."

"Where are the Ancient Hebrews now?" said Valerie, sniffling a bit.

"They're all dead," said Benjamin.

"Good," said Valerie.

There was no reason for Benjamin to be feeling guilty but he did. He didn't like the feeling but he just couldn't seem to shake it. He'd never felt guilty before. That was probably because he'd never had a friend before.

"But Benjamin dear, it's so *dreadfully* unfair. You see how clean I am. If you place any animal or any person inside a pen and keep them locked up inside, they will become dirty, too. Surely you see that, dear Benjamin."

"Valerie, as a friend I would put you in the nativity scene. As an artist, I cannot."

"Oh, Benjamin," cried Valerie, "my mind understands but my heart does not. I thought we were friends."

At this point, she turned away from the boy and broke down into deep, uncontrollable sobbing. Benjamin did not know what to do or say. For the first time in his life he felt something break inside his heart.

"Please stop crying, dear Valerie," he said.

But the pig did not stop crying. And Benjamin felt very sad, indeed.

"Valerie, dear," he said at last. "No friend is worth your tears except the one who never makes you cry."

CHAPTER SEVENTEEN

The Dog, the Cat, and the Three Wise Men

HITCHCOCK THE ROOSTER found his place on the canvas and the days and nights went by, but things did not feel quite the same to Benjamin. Valerie pretended like nothing had happened but she seemed colder and older and she wasn't eating very well. She would occasionally offer a supportive comment here and there to the young artist, but you could tell her heart wasn't really in it. Her mind was still as sharp as ever, for instance, when she pointed out to Benjamin that the dog and the cat were not true barnyard animals and hence should not be included in a traditional por-

117

trayal of the manger. But Benjamin was rushing now and felt limited as to what he had to work with, and he plowed right ahead placing Sambo the dog and Cuddles the cat into the adoring circle of animals surrounding the Baby Jesus.

The work itself was really starting to take shape. Even Valerie had to admit that. All that was left were the three wise men and Jesus, Joseph, and Mary, of course, and there was still one week to go, always allowing for the time it'd take to deliver the finished art to Eddystone Castle.

Benjamin felt many new emotions coursing through his young soul, feelings he never remembered feeling before. He felt good, he felt tired, he felt exhilarated, and he felt kind of sad about Valerie. But Valerie, true to her strong feminine nature, put up a brave front. She was determined not to let any man, even a ten-year-old, get the best of her. Inside, however, her heart had yet not come to terms with being excluded from Benjamin's art. There was still hope, of course. It was a work in progress. There was yet a little time for a friend to change his mind.

"It feels like a very cold night," said Benjamin,

looking around for Valerie, as he pulled the quilt a bit tighter around his shoulders. But Valerie didn't answer. Benjamin was having a minor technical problem fitting the three wise men into the entrance to the manger. He had a fairly good idea what they would look like if he could just get them there.

"Valerie dear," he called again. Still, there was no answer.

Benjamin took the lantern and walked over to the pigpen. There was Valerie sound asleep in the hay and the dirt of the cold floor of the barn. The door to the pen was closed and he wondered if she'd closed it herself because she wanted to be alone. This worried Benjamin. Valerie had previously taken such a great pride and interest in his work. Surely she knew by now that he would have put her in the manger if he could.

Valerie stirred slightly and Benjamin noticed that she was shivering. When she opened her eyes to look at him, there was a certain sadness there he hadn't seen before.

"Dear Valerie," he said. "You're shivering. Take my quilt. It'll help keep you warm."

"Dear Benjamin," she said. "There's only so much warmth and love in this world and there's never enough to go around. Pigs don't need quilts. Pigs need people to understand them."

"I understand you, dear Valerie."

"I know you do, Benjamin dear," she said, as she closed her eyes and went back to sleep.

Benjamin went back to his easel and went back to work on the wise men. After a while, he'd sketched them in to his satisfaction but he found he missed Valerie's little nods of approval and the twinkle of encouragement for a job well done that now and then he could see in her eyes. Ah well, he thought, an artist's life is often meant to be a lonely one. He'd never minded before working alone in his room or working alone in the barn by lantern light. But then he'd never had a friend before. And he'd never missed a friend before.

In a strange way, he thought, Valerie had not only helped him perfect his art, she'd also helped him discover himself.

Dawn was but a few hours away when the boy put his brush down and stood back to take a critical look at his rendering of the three wise men bearing their gifts for the babe in the manger. Benjamin had drawn them from memory. The first wise man was Will Wallace, the farmhand. The second wise man was the Viking. The third wise man was a little memorial from the artist to the now deceased White Knight. The work was nearing completion, Benjamin figured. All that was lacking was Jesus, Joseph, and Mary, give or take a few shepherds, if needed for balance and composition. All in all, the artist felt quite satisfied with the quality of the work. He also felt confident that he would have the commission completed on time.

But as talented an artist as Benjamin may have been, he was still a ten-year-old boy, and ten-year-old boys are not always the most accurate barometers of life. The lad was far more exhausted than, indeed, he realized. He sat down in the chair and leaned back to rest for a moment and the next thing he knew he was sound asleep.

Benjamin was dreaming that he and Valerie were

aboard a ship at the wheel of which was the Viking. They were sailing in peaceful aquamarine waters enjoying the warm sunshine on the deck. He and Valerie were happy and smiling and discussing Leonardo Da Vinci's painting of *The Last Supper*.

"You may not be aware of this, dear Benjamin," Valerie was saying, "but it took Da Vinci almost as long as Jesus lived for him to complete *The Last Supper*."

"He obviously wasn't working for the king," said Benjamin.

Valerie laughed. It felt nice to see her laughing again.

"Da Vinci used his friends as models for the disciples," Valerie continued. "But Jesus and Judas were the two centerpieces of the work and he could not readily find suitable models for them. So one day he saw a young man at the university who had quite a beatific face and Da Vinci thought he'd be perfect for the face of Jesus. He asked the young man if he would sit for him and the man said yes and so he did.

"Da Vinci, much like you, dear Benjamin, did not realize that his work would become a great master-

piece. So he put it away for almost thirty years because he couldn't find the perfect face for Judas. He
was working on other things, of course."

"Of course," said Benjamin. Valerie was probably
the smartest pig in the world, thought Benjamin. It
felt so peaceful and comforting to be gently rocking
on the waves and listening to her talk about Da
Vinci.

"Anyway," continued Valerie, "now it's thirty years
later and he's on the street in Rome and he sees a
guy with the perfect face for Judas. Not evil or ugly,
but kind of seductive and soft. So he catches up with
the guy and asks the fellow if he'll sit for him. The
man says yes, but then he says, 'You don't remember
me, but I sat for you thirty years ago. I was the face
of Jesus.' "

"That was a wonderful story, dear Valerie," said
Benjamin, as he lay back on the gently rolling deck
of the ship and let the golden rays of the sun warm
his very being. "But is the story true?"

"Oh, yes, dear Benjamin," said Valerie. "The part
about Da Vinci is true. The application of the story
to the lives of all of us is, sadly, even truer."

"Valerie, dear," said Benjamin. "I think you must be the smartest pig in the world."

"Of course I am, dear Benjamin," she said. "I chose you to be my friend."

A man who looked very much like Feinberg, the king's advisor, came out on deck with a tray of cold drinks for Valerie and Benjamin. "For madame and monsieur," he said. Then the Viking shouted: "Land ho! Off the starboard bow!" And they saw a lovely tropical island with sand and thatched huts and palm trees and beautiful birds of all the colors of the rainbow. The boy wished the voyage could go on forever. It was very much like life itself, he thought. Beautiful, a bit rough sometimes, and interesting.

A volcano erupted on the island sending shimmering sparks into the sky. Benjamin could see the sparks reflecting in Valerie's eyes. It was so nice to be with someone you wanted to be with.

And still the boy slept. And still the boy dreamed. And the barn was on fire.

CHAPTER EIGHTEEN

Jesus, Joseph, and Mary

IT IS SAD BUT TRUE that people and animals in real life rarely comport themselves as they are often portrayed in art. It would have been nice to believe that Jezebel the noble white steed might come galloping through the flames to the rescue. But she did not. She huddled in a far corner of the barn without giving forth with so much as a whinny to wake the boy. Nell the cow stood mute with her eyes in a dull glaze. The lamb was nowhere to be seen. The rooster did not crow. The dog was asleep. The cat had gotten out of the barn to save her own hide at the first sign of flames. There were no wise men standing at the door ready to come to the rescue. There was only a lantern that had fallen off an easel in an old barn in the dark before the dawn. And there was an extremely exhausted little boy with a quilt wrapped tightly around him, still sound asleep in his chair.

The story could have ended there and by all rights it probably should have. Dreams come to an end every moment of every day and night, and one way or another, dreamers always seem to awaken to a world unfortunately unpopulated by wise men and talking pigs.

As the smoke and flames billowed up in the middle of the barn floor, tongues of fire began eating through the scattered hay in multiple directions. One of those pathways of flame would very soon be blocking the doorway to the barn. It was at this fateful moment that the boy felt the quilt being suddenly pulled away from him. He tried to pull it back around him. He felt a sharp nudge in his ribs. He heard Valerie's voice screaming. It would have been impossible for anyone who heard that sound not to wake up. And finally, because of the heroic actions of one brave pig, he did.

Benjamin attempted partially successfully to

smother the genesis of the fire with the thick comforter his aunt had provided him. He ran to the water trough and started to throw buckets of water on the expanding flames. The animals, with the notable exception of Valerie, were now all wide awake and panicking in the smoky barn. The pig stood valiantly by the easel, as if preparing to make a last stand to protect the painting.

At this dire moment, Will Wallace, having risen early to do the farm chores, smelled the smoke and came bursting into the barn. For the next few moments Will and Benjamin fought a pitched battle with the flames while the animals raced around the barn in crazy circles like a frenzied carousel of death. The man and the boy repeatedly doused the smoldering flames with bucket after bucket of water from the trough. The fire was all but extinguished by the time Uncle Floyd and Aunt Joan came running into the barn.

The first thing that happened was something that no one there had expected to see. It was a unique occurrence that had never transpired before. It was Aunt Joan and Benjamin embracing each other. Valerie nodded her head approvingly, but in all the excitement and emotion, of course, nobody really paid much notice to the pig. But Valerie, being her usual modest self, fully realized what she'd done. She'd not only saved the boy's life, but she'd done her part in helping to bring him out of that lonely, terrible shell in which he'd been living.

"Thank God you boys put out the fire before anyone was hurt," said Uncle Floyd. "The painting appears to be undamaged. Very fine work, Benjamin. We've just been informed by special courier, however, that the piece must be ready to be picked up three full days before Christmas. The roads are uncertain at this time of year, and the king wants to take no chances on the painting arriving late to Eddystone Castle. That leaves but two days to complete the effort. You can do it, lad. I know you can."

"Surely you're not serious," said Aunt Joan. "You can see the exhausted state Benjamin is in. He can barely hold his head up. And no more working alone in the barn late at night, young man."

"Darling," said Uncle Floyd. "You must not let your heart take dominance over your head. The lad is a lad but he's also an artist! He has but two days remaining to complete his art. For the sake of us all, he may have to work day *and* night."

"I don't like it, Floyd. It's too dangerous. I don't want him working alone all night in this barn."

"All right," said Uncle Floyd. "Then I'll stay here at the barn all night with him if necessary. The work must be finished on time."

After that, things settled down a bit. Floyd and Will stayed around to clean up the debris caused by the fire. Aunt Joan went into the house with Benjamin to cook him his oatmeal. And Valerie? She trotted quietly back to her pen and, looking like any other pig in the world, she lay there alone in the mud.

⚫   ⚫   ⚫

Will Wallace, after he'd finished admiring his depiction as one of the three wise men, did not feel so wise just at the moment. What Floyd had said seemed right to him. The boy was an artist and his job was to complete the painting on time. Otherwise the farm would be lost. Yet what Joan had said also seemed right to Will Wallace. It was unhealthy and unwise to allow the boy to push himself so hard. He was already in a state of exhaustion. Let the kid rest.

Will Wallace wondered how it was possible that Floyd and Joan could hold such diametrically opposite opinions on the subject. Yet what the boy's uncle had said was right. And yet what the boy's aunt had said was also right. "How could they *both* be right?" he asked himself. He didn't know it, but he was right, too.

And late that night in the deserted barn the easel stood alone in the cold, leftover moonlight. Valerie stood alone, too, wistfully gazing at the unfinished work of art. It no longer bothered her so much that the painting included every animal in the barn except herself. Life, she knew, was merely a series of disappointments, an accumulation of losses. Whether one was a pig or a person, sometimes there was nothing to do but wallow in the mud and the grime that were the brick and the mortar of the road that was the journey of life.

They're all waiting for the Christ child, Valerie thought to herself.

And, indeed, she was right. Every animal appeared to be watching the blank center of the canvas for the babe in the manger to appear. The wise men stood at the door waiting expectantly for the empty space in the middle to fill up with glory, and sweetness, and hope. And outside the barn, thought Valerie, it was just the same. Every living being was waiting for love.

Valerie suddenly felt very lonely. She'd heard what Benjamin's uncle had said and what his aunt had said and she knew that she and the boy might never be alone in the barn again. Their nocturnal conversations had been a thing of joy to Valerie and now they may have come to an end. In truth, she missed Benjamin very much. She knew that he was a boy. She knew that she was a pig. But they'd been such good friends.

●   ●   ●

Benjamin did not return that day. And, though Valerie waited up for him, he did not come back that night. In fact, it wasn't until the following morning that Benjamin, accompanied by his uncle, walked into the barn in a very brusque and businesslike fashion, sat down at the easel, and began mixing some paints for his final assault on the canvas. As far as Benjamin was concerned, his mind was now in rather of a jumble. All the pressure of a lifetime lived in silence, of having to be the family's breadwinner at age ten, of a dream interrupted by a fire, almost made him wonder if the whole thing hadn't been a dream. In the bright, cold light of the new day, that certainly seemed like a possibility. He almost didn't want to find out. It would be like finding out that life was but a dream. And besides, right now he didn't have the time.

Benjamin began painting like a boy with his hair on fire, which, indeed, had almost happened quite literally two nights before. To him, his uncle wasn't there, none of the animals were there, nothing was there but the brush and the canvas. He'd never spoken before he'd met Valerie, he thought, and perhaps he might never speak again. Maybe the fire had caused a certain kind of damage that could not readily be seen or identified. Maybe it had destroyed a dream.

Uncle Floyd, though he'd become quite adept at carrying on one-way conversations with the lad, was somewhat reverential about interrupting his genius at work. As a farmer, he was not a big talker anyway. He maintained silence now as he went about preparing to milk the cow. Nor did Valerie even bother to come out of her pen. With the uncle there in the bright daylight, and the boy in a seeming daze of sorts, perhaps the magic was gone. Maybe Cuddles the cat had got her tongue, she thought. She realized that she and Benjamin were not, of course, star-crossed lovers like Romeo and Juliet. Maybe they were something even sadder. Maybe they were star-crossed friends.

To Benjamin, completing the canvas felt very much like chopping wood or performing some other mundane farm chore. He was quite possibly unaware of the fact but many great artists have described their work similarly. Flashes of brilliance are few and far between, and often they go unrecognized by the artist himself. They are only spotted many years later by the eye of the critic or the casual viewer.

In what seemed like an incredibly short period of time, the painting was complete and Benjamin had left the building. He was bound for his bowl of oatmeal by the time his uncle, carrying a bucket of milk, walked over to the easel to peruse the boy's work. Predictably perhaps, the farmer and his wife had been pressed into action as Joseph and Mary. They seemed to look the part, the farmer thought, all things considered.

The Baby Jesus, he recognized, was identical to the long-ago-lost doll that he himself had once given the boy. The farmer was not a professor of psychic phenomena, but he appreciated the fact that most young boys would not have an eidetic memory of a doll that had disappeared before they were two. Though the farmer probably did not see things quite that way, it could be said that because of Benjamin's unique affliction, his childhood had very possibly vanished not long after the doll.

As a certain pig had once observed, life was an accumulation of losses.

CHAPTER NINETEEN

A Christmas Pig

THAT NIGHT, ONCE AGAIN, the boy felt like a dreamer who could not sleep. Was his life all a dream? he wondered. Valerie? Visiting the king? The royal commission? The fire in the barn? Would he ever wake up and be like other people? When he conducted magical conversations with a pig, was that a dream, too? Or was everything else a dream? He had no answers, only questions. And the final question was: What use were dreams if all they ever did was come true?

In an even larger sense, however, Benjamin was well aware that something strange was happening to him. For better or worse, he was slowly but surely awakening to the world around him. This could only be a bad thing if the world was bad, he thought. Part of him did not want to find out. But a far bigger, deeper part of him had felt oddly comforted when he'd embraced Aunt Joan after the fire. And talking to Valerie may all have been some kind of crazy dream, but at least it had been a happy one. With all his young heart he did not want it to be a dream but perhaps, like everything else, it was.

Now Benjamin comforted his troubled soul by listening to the murmurings of his aunt and uncle in their nearby room. They sounded like a waterfall in a peaceful garden. He loved to hear their murmurings.

"Will Wallace has told me an interesting story," his uncle was saying. "He says that he's been hearing strange voices in the barn late at night this past week."

"Really, dear. That *is* strange."

"Will Wallace says that one of the voices sounded very much like that of a young boy. He believes the voice was Benjamin's."

"Good Lord!"

"That's what I said to Will Wallace."

"Do you think we should have a doctor look at him?"

"Look at who?"

"Will Wallace, of course. Benjamin's never spoken in his life. Why should Will Wallace be hearing him now?"

"I can't answer that one," said the uncle.

"If Will Wallace is hearing voices, this could be very serious. Joan of Arc heard voices and look what happened to her."

Benjamin liked Joan of Arc. He did not like what had happened to her. But he was very excited to learn that Will Wallace had heard voices. So it hadn't been a dream after all. The murmuring was silent for a while. Then the boy could hear it again.

"There has been a change in Benjamin," said Aunt Joan thoughtfully. "One of the most precious moments in my life was when he came into my arms after the fire in the barn. That was a lovely experience."

"The lad did a beautiful job completing the nativity scene, as well," said his uncle. "Damn fine effort.

You and I, perhaps you'd like to know, are officially presented as Mary and Joseph."

"How thoughtful of Benjamin."

"He's a thoughtful lad. He's a talented lad. If he could only just—"

"Don't get into it now, Floyd. He is what he is. Benjamin is Benjamin and we're very lucky to have him."

"I couldn't agree more, darling."

Benjamin did not like the murmurings so much when they were murmurings about him. It made him a bit uncomfortable to be hearing about himself. He preferred to just be able to sit inside the waterfall and listen to the magical, musical messages murmuring all about him. At the moment, however, there was silence again. Silence and more silence. He tossed and turned in his bed, unable to sleep, unable to dream, unable to clear his head of odd thoughts. One of them was that the murmuring reminded him rather fondly of Valerie when she spoke to him. At long last, the sounds commenced again.

"Did I tell you," his uncle was saying, "that I received word from Long Lama today that the courier from Eddystone Castle is scheduled to arrive in the morning? He is to deliver the painting to the court. In the event that I am in the barn or the field when he arrives, please alert me. I'd like to be on hand when the art is transferred into his custody."

"Of course, darling. What does the babe in the manger look like?"

"It is the spitting image of that little doll I gave the lad back when he, too, was practically a babe in a manger."

"That little doll of Benjamin's," said Aunt Joan dreamily. "I'd all but forgotten that little doll."

"Yes, well that little bugger has now been resurrected as the Lamb of God."

"Floyd!"

"Well, it's true. And a fine-looking babe he is."

"I think we should be very proud of Benjamin," said Aunt Joan. "If the king's commission is a generous one, the boy may well have saved the farm. Not only that, but if the unveiling of the painting at the midnight mass is successfully received, he might just become the most famous artist in the kingdom!"

"I don't think Benjamin really wants fame, though."

"I know what he really wants," said his aunt. "He wants to be just like any other normal ten-year-old boy."

"Well, he's not," said Uncle Floyd. "Let's not discuss matters we have no control over. Right at the moment he's the family breadwinner and that's a lot to ask of even someone my age. It's never an easy life trying to support a family as a farmer."

"You've done fine, darling."

"I've done fine except that without Benjamin we'd lose this farm."

"Don't be hard on yourself, Floyd. You've always worked hard and you've done your best and that's all anybody can ask of anybody."

"I suppose. There is one piece of good news, however, as far as our finances go. Do you remember Lord Myers of Keswick, the nice nobleman who escorted Benjamin and myself back home from the court?"

"Why, yes, dear. What about him?"

"You recall he took a stroll with me through the barnyard when he was here?"

"Yes."

"Well, he wants a Christmas pig to roast for his family. He's prepared to pay a fine price for our pig and he's suggested that the royal couriers could pick her up tomorrow morning when they come to get the painting."

"But, darling," said Aunt Joan. "That pig is so small and so young."

"In today's market, small young pigs are considered the most succulent. I don't feel good about getting rid of the pig either, but that's what we raise them for."

"I know we need the money, darling, but—"

"Don't fret yourself," said Uncle Floyd. "The animal will not be slaughtered here. The couriers will see that it is done before they reach the court. They'll see that everything is taken care of."

"Well—"

"Now, now, it's all settled. They'll be here in the morning to fetch the painting and the pig."

"Good night, darling."

"Good night, dear."

CHAPTER TWENTY

An Empty Canvas

THE BOY DID NOT SLEEP. He could not sleep. He wanted to cry but he did not. He never cried. Besides, there was work to be done. All he required was an empty canvas. As empty as the whole world. He waited until he was sure his uncle and his aunt had gone to sleep. Then, under cover of darkness and grief, he slipped out of the house and crept over to the barn.

"Benjamin?" came a familiar voice in the blackness of the old building.

"Yes, Valerie," said the boy. "It's me."

"Dear, dear Benjamin," she said. "Why have you come here?"

"I cannot tell you, dear Valerie. But I will show you soon. There is very little time so just let me paint."

"I thought your work was finished."

"No, dear Valerie," he said. "My work has just begun."

With that, he moved determinedly to the easel, lit the lanterns very carefully this time, and lifted the canvas off the easel. It was a large canvas and he was a small boy, but he managed to quickly turn it around and place it back on the easel so the blank back of the canvas was facing him. He opened the paints, mixed them to his satisfaction, and then, using no subjects or models, began painting from memory, from the heights of genius, from the depths of his soul.

Outside the barn, the weather had taken a decided turn for the worse. The wind was blowing shrilly from the north and snow and ice had begun to blanket the little farm and the forest nearby. Benjamin wielded the brush with a power and determination equal to the elements outside. For inside his heart, another storm was raging.

At one point, standing now, darting back and forth and side to side, splashing colors and forms frenetically across the canvas with flying brushstrokes, Valerie had come into his little circle of light. When she looked at him she saw something in his eyes that she'd never seen before but always suspected was there, the fear and guts of true courage.

"Go back! Go back, Valerie, dear," he said, without interrupting the rhythm of his work. "We have so little time. I'll show you when I'm done."

"Yes, dear Benjamin," she said, as she walked back to her pen. "I will do as you say. For you have become the artist of my life."

Benjamin may have heard words or he may not have, for he was in a world of his own, much the way he'd existed for most of his life, except now it was focused into a fleeting few hours, into a feverish fugue of finality and freedom. The back of the canvas was coming to life with a masterpiece in the making. The front of the canvas had taken him two or three weeks to paint. It was good. But the back of the canvas had taken him only a few hours to paint. It was not merely good; it was great. For it had been painted with colors that most artists never used. Colors like no time to lose, nowhere to run, and love is never lost. The empty canvas was now full of all the words that Benjamin had never spoken, all the emotions that Benjamin had never felt.

"Valerie!" he called. "Dear Valerie! The painting is finished. I want you to be the first one to see it."

As Valerie trotted over to view the work, the boy pulled the quilt ever more tightly around his shoulders. It was, indeed, an extremely cold night. Soon, he knew, it would get even colder.

When Valerie saw the painting, she became almost as speechless as Benjamin had been before he'd met her. A small tear formed in the corner of her eye and fell to the floor.

"What do you think?" asked Benjamin.

"It's the most beautiful thing I've seen in my life," she said at last. "Except for your soul."

It was sometime in the early hours of the morning when the boy completed the final preparations for the painting to be received by the royal couriers the next day. This involved painting over the original work, which was now on the back side of the canvas.

146

This task Benjamin performed quickly, and seemingly with little regret. Lastly, he removed from a box the royal purple velvet curtain that had been sent from the castle along with the canvas and art supplies. He fitted the curtain onto the frame and attached it in such a way as to keep the contents of the painting a mystery until the time for it to be formally unveiled. This proved to be a rather meticulous process, not unlike the hooking up of a fancy ball gown.

Valerie watched from the cold dirt floor of the barn, her eyes sparkling in the candlelight cast by the lanterns. Indeed, she appeared almost to radiate a joy of spirit and a peace of mind she had never before experienced in her brief young life. That the boy would risk the commission and the king's displeasure by including her in the painting, meant the world to her. For it had taken worldsful of courage, she knew. Worldsful of courage and perhaps something even harder to find, true friendship.

Finally, the painting was veiled with the velvet curtain, wrapped once again for travel, and, on that lonely easel in that creaky old barn, stood waiting for destiny. Benjamin blew out the lanterns and, with the warm quilt around his body, walked to the door of the barn. As he opened the door he noticed that the weather had gone from bad to worse. The snow was piling up on the ground in large drifts and in many places seemed to be turning to ice. And still it kept falling from the gray, oblivious sky.

"Good night, dear Benjamin," said Valerie.

"You're coming with me," he said.

CHAPTER TWENTY-ONE

The Forest

DAWN NEVER CAME that morning. Instead, the canvas of the world was permeated with an aching off-whiteness that smothered the senses and dulled the spirit. It was a rather unique and isolated weather pattern, however. The four royal couriers from Eddystone Castle did not encounter the icy weather until they'd crossed the little wooden bridge on the way to the farm.

When the king's men reached the Welches' farmhouse that morning, Aunt Joan was waiting with hot tea for them all. Afterward, Uncle Floyd went with them to the barn and formally turned over to them the painting, which they promptly loaded onto the covered cart.

When the men returned to the barn to collect the pig, they were rather surprised to find that the pen was empty. With Uncle Floyd and Will Wallace leading the way, every nook and cranny of the old building was searched and scrutinized but the pig was not found. Uncle Floyd was baffled and a bit disappointed by the experience, but when he told his wife about the disappearance later that morning, she said, "Good for the pig." Benjamin, it was assumed, was still asleep in his bedroom. He was not.

As the artist's rendering of the babe in the manger rolled inexorably toward Eddystone Castle, the couriers remarked on how the weather had improved. This was not the case, however, in the northern portion of the kingdom. Here, the wind shrieked, the snow kept coming, and everything on the ground turned almost instantly to ice. Some would later claim that it was the worst blizzard to hit the north in over a hundred years.

In the middle of this terrible storm, a small boy

and a pig walked blameless into a snowbound forest primeval where day was night and night was cold and the angry wind whistled through the branches in the dense canopy of trees that hid the gray cathedral sky. Benjamin liked the dark and gray colors all around him but he had not been prepared for a storm of this magnitude. Valerie, who was better suited for the cold than the boy, worried about him with nothing but the quilt and the clothes on his back. It had been the boy's plan to get as far away from the farm as possible, but soon they were lost amidst the drifts of swirling snow.

They walked for many hours through the forest with wolves howling in the distance, and then seemingly closer and closer. Predatory fingers of ice dripped from branches and pointed in every direction but home. That was fine with Benjamin. He was not going home.

After several more hours of wandering, they stopped in a small clearing and Benjamin tried to build a fire with some matches he'd brought. This was not an easy task in the cold and wet forest, but at last he succeeded. The two of them talked quietly and tried to warm themselves by the small campfire.

Other voices, by now, were calling as well. Uncle Floyd and Aunt Joan and Will Wallace had been scouring the woods, calling for Benjamin. These cries, however, had been deadened by the deep, still falling snow, and the wind and the wolves. The boy, both freezing and exhausted, began to shiver violently.

"Oh, dear Benjamin," said Valerie at last, "we must go back."

"If we go back, dear Valerie," he said, "they will kill you."

"But you've already saved me," she said. "You've put me in the painting. For that, I will be eternally grateful. Eternally grateful, oh, dear, dear Benjamin."

Hearing her words, Benjamin did something he'd never done in his life. He began to cry.

"I don't want to lose you, dear Valerie," he sobbed. "You're my only friend."

"No friend is worth your tears," she said, "except the one who never makes you cry."

No one knows how long they remained there, how long the fire lasted. It could have been a day or a lifetime. The temperature dropped steadily. The snow and ice kept falling from a sky they could no longer see. The boy at last fell asleep and Valerie curled up next to him to try to keep him warm. But she could not keep him warm enough.

They say that pigs are smarter than dogs and just as loyal, though, of course, they have a lot less reason to be. This having been said, a pig can survive in the cold and wild for far longer than a small boy. That is, if the pig wants to. In this case, the pig chose to remain next to the boy's still warm body, and if necessary, die by his side. Which is exactly what she did.

Thus it was that snowflakes soon covered Valerie's delicate eyelashes. Thus it was that on the day Jesus was born, Benjamin died.

CHAPTER TWENTY-TWO

The Midnight Mass

FEINBERG WAS NERVOUS. The midnight mass was winding to a close in the great hall of Eddystone Castle and Feinberg was pacing briskly back and forth behind the biggest crowd he'd ever seen in his life. It seemed the whole kingdom had turned out to watch the velvet draperies drop from Benjamin's painting, which was now situated high on the castle wall behind the priest. Rumors had coursed through the populace, apparently, that this nativity scene was the work of a child painting a child. Not only that, but this particular child was a ten-year-old idiot savant from the north country.

Feinberg remembered with a shudder the child-like, primitive, grotesque monstrosity the kid had painted for him when the boy had spent the night at Eddystone Castle. Another performance like that, thought Feinberg, and we'll all be out of business. In keeping with the traditions of the midnight mass, no human eye had seen the painting except the artist himself. Not the king. Not Feinberg. No one could say for sure what was behind that velvet curtain. It was one tradition, thought Feinberg, that he could do without.

Feinberg had a plan, of course. He always had a plan. If things went terribly wrong and the crowd hated the painting, he would leap to prominence in the room, jump in front of the parade, and take a leadership position in reviling the work. There was at least a fair chance, in that event, that King Jonjo might not remember Feinberg's instrumental role in granting the royal commission to the kid in the first place.

Suddenly, the church bells were ringing and the Christmas Eve midnight mass was over and, for the first time in his life, Feinberg found himself praying. Dear God, he prayed, let the king love the painting!

Let the people love the painting! Let the world not blame Feinberg!

The prayer appeared to be just in time, for King Jonjo was now making his way from his royal throne to the pulpit. The king was decked out in a very royal purple robe, his crown flashing in the torch-light, and his scepter seemingly covered with, well, fireflies. The king's taking the proscenium made a very pretty picture, indeed. Feinberg hoped with all his heart that there was also a very pretty picture lurking inside the velvet drapery on the wall behind the king.

And then the king waved his scepter, and the trumpets blew, and two knights stepped to either side of the painting and, with great ceremonial flourish, removed the curtain. The crowd stared in stunned silence. For the painting included no Joseph, no Mary, no shepherds, and no wise men. It was comprised entirely of a distant circle of animals and two beautifully drawn centerpieces that dominated the work. One of these was the Baby Jesus on a bale of hay. The other centerpiece, with its hooves up on the hay and its head pressed perilously close

157

to the future Savior of the world, was a pig. If that were not enough, one of the Christ child's little hands extended lovingly to touch the pig's adoring face.

It did not take long for the catcalls and the heckling to start. Soon the entire multitude was openly mocking the painting and calling for the head of the artist. As the mood of the crowd grew uglier, Feinberg leapt to the fore, vigorously employing plan B.

"It's blasphemous!" he shouted. "It's sacrilege! It's not kosher!"

Meanwhile, King Jonjo stepped to the front of the stage and violently wielded his scepter. The crowd quieted rapidly, then hushed to total silence. Then the king, in possibly his finest hour, spoke thusly to the crowd:

"My people," he said. "Do you not see what this artist is trying to tell us? He is providing us an indication of the kind of man this babe would grow up to be. A man who would love and embrace lepers and prisoners and prostitutes and, yes, pigs. Can you not see that this young man's work is worthy of the loving spirit of the King of Kings? This is a great painting, I tell you. It is a work of art that shall for-ever be cherished in the hearts of men."

The crowd began applauding rather tentatively, then swelled into hearty cheers and newfound adulation for the painting. Feinberg, again, was quite prominent in leading the worshipful response.

"It's brilliant!" shouted Feinberg. "It's a master-piece! What was I thinking? I must have had a nail in my head."

"Now you see," said the king to the crowd. "Now you know."

CHAPTER TWENTY-THREE

The Angels

AND GOD CALLED about Him a band of angels. And He said, "Bring me two shining stars." And the angels weren't quite sure what He meant so they got together a little focus group.

"What's the Old Man talking about?" said the angel named Tom Baker. "We can't bring him two stars."

"Don't be ridiculous," said the angel named Kacey Cohen. "He's just speaking metaphorically again."

So the angels decided they would find the two most shining spirits in all the earth. They had been watching mortal events unfold, so they went directly to the forest and found the little frozen bodies of the young boy and the pig. These they wrapped in gossamer and took back before God's throne.

"Bingo!" said God to the angels. "This young boy shall forever paint in My mansion of peace, and this young pig shall forever romp in its hallways of happiness. And both of them shall be by My side for all eternity.

"Furthermore," said God, "on either side of that star that led the wise men to Jesus, I shall place two other stars. One will be for Benjamin, and one will be for Valerie.

"And though men may later call these three stars in a line Orion's Belt, they are placed by *My* hand for a purpose. And that is to lead men, women, children, and animals to the light forevermore."

KINKY FRIEDMAN lives in a little green trailer somewhere in the hills of Texas. He has five dogs, one armadillo, and one Smith-Corona typewriter. By the time you are reading this, Mr. Friedman may either be celebrating becoming the next governor of Texas or he may have retired in a petulant snit.

Printed in the United States
By Bookmasters